Grant could still remember the first time he'd seen her.

She'd glanced at him over her shoulder with that sunny, innocent smile, and he'd been lost.

Memories and fairy tales, he reminded himself as he moved to the glass wall of his office with purposeful strides and gazed down at the bustling streets of New York City.

No, he'd made real progress after he'd accepted that Alexandra had used and discarded him. He'd accrued his first million before he was thirty and now stood on the cusp of becoming a billionaire before he was thirty-five.

He turned back toward his desk, the unique floral arrangement catching his eye. It was striking, and despite the person behind the proposal, she'd made a good pitch.

That he had the upper hand this time certainly didn't hurt. In fact, he thought as he turned the possibility around in his mind, hiring Alexandra would serve two purposes. Adding a little extra class to the upcoming events, yes, but also showing her exactly what she had thrown away.

Emmy Grayson wrote her first book at the age of seven about a spooky ghost. Her passion for romance novels began a few years later with the discovery of a worn copy of Kathleen Woodiwiss's *A Rose in Winter* buried on her mother's bookshelf. She lives in the Midwest countryside with her husband (who's also her ex-husband), their children and enough animals to start their own zoo.

Books by Emmy Grayson

Harlequin Presents

The Infamous Cabrera Brothers

His Billion-Dollar Takeover Temptation
Proof of Their One Hot Night
A Deal for the Tycoon's Diamonds

The Van Ambrose Royals

A Cinderella for the Prince's Revenge
The Prince's Pregnant Secretary

Visit the Author Profile page at Harlequin.com.

Emmy Grayson

CINDERELLA HIRED FOR HIS REVENGE

HARLEQUIN
PRESENTS

HARLEQUIN®
PRESENTS™

ISBN-13: 978-1-335-73907-0

Cinderella Hired for His Revenge

Copyright © 2023 by Emmy Grayson

For questions and comments about the quality of this book,
please contact us at CustomerService@Harlequin.com.

Harlequin Enterprises ULC
22 Adelaide St. West, 41st Floor
Toronto, Ontario M5H 4E3, Canada
www.Harlequin.com

Printed in U.S.A.

CINDERELLA HIRED
FOR HIS REVENGE

To my husband and my children with love, with a special note of thanks to my new baby girl, who got me up at 1:00 a.m., 3:00 a.m. and 5:00 a.m. for two weeks to make sure I had time to finish this book.

CHAPTER ONE

ALEXANDRA MOSS GAZED out over Central Park, her eyes drinking in the welcome signs that spring had finally arrived: bright green grass, rosy-pink blossoms on the cherry trees, sidewalks crowded with joggers, bikers and families. Winter had held on to New York City with a vicious, icy grip through the end of March. But finally, the sun had started to beat back the gray clouds, and spring had arrived in all her beautiful, colorful glory last week.

Alexandra's fingers tightened on the black leather sport folio clutched in her hands. Just in time for the final nail to be hammered into her coffin. Her landlord had raised the rent on her little shop in SoHo the same day her biggest client, a bride with a soap opera star for a mother, decided to elope and canceled her entire floral order. It was enough of a financial setback that she'd had to let her part-time employee, Sylvia, go, leaving her working sunup to sundown to make the arrangements, monitor online orders, manage social media and oversee everything else that came with running a floral store in New York City.

Ten thousand dollars, minus a one-thousand-dollar deposit, gone in the blink of an eye. That and a chance to show The Flower Bell was capable of handling the exclusive, high-priced events that would keep her store running.

She turned away from the floor-to-ceiling windows and faced down the empty mahogany conference table. No chairs yet, or any other furniture. The up-and-coming Pearson Group had just moved into the forty-sixth floor of the Carlson, an exclusive building that hosted the offices of public relations firms, ad agencies and financial organizations like Pearson.

When her friend Pamela, a manager with a luxury catering company, had suggested trying to land a corporate contract, Alexandra had hesitated. She'd done some work for businesses in her college internship, but she'd always imagined weddings, baby showers and anniversary parties when she'd thought of the types of events The Flower Bell would service. But the more she'd thought about it, the challenge and the change of pace, she'd decided to go for it. Pamela had snuck her a list of companies with upcoming events.

The first thing Alexandra had done was scour it for any familiar names. It had been seven years since her father, David Waldsworth, had landed in prison after his pyramid scheme had collapsed. The majority of the victims had been blue-collar workers and middle-class families. A point the media had used to hammer her family into the ground, with phrases like, "There's no way they could have not known," plaguing her throughout the trial wherever she went. She'd started buying clothes at thrift stores the week after the trial, unable to bear the thought that her silk blouses and sheath dresses had been purchased with a military veteran's savings or a grandmother's meager retirement fund. Most of her and the family's belongings, including the penthouse, the private plane, the house in the Hamptons and the seaside home on Martha's Vineyard, had been sold to cover her father's debts and start a victims' compensation fund. A fund that even now was several hundred million short of the amount her father had stolen.

Her stepmother had cried but Alexandra had breathed a sigh of relief, grateful to have the reminders of what David's perfidy had bought gone.

Now, after nine years of rebuilding herself, she was once again on the verge of losing everything.

But you won't, she told herself firmly as she breathed in deeply. *You're going to land another contract and The Flower Bell will be a success.*

She'd been nervous about approaching the Pearson Group. It sounded exactly like the kind of firm David had been trying to build his company into, except he'd built it on the backs of hardworking people who had trusted him. All to keep the family name among the elite of New York society after he'd squandered the Waldsworth fortune.

Plenty of people in those upper circles remembered the scandal. However, Pamela had mentioned that the new CEO had recently moved to New York from Los Angeles and so she needed to take the risk. The worst that could happen was that she could get escorted out by security. The best was that she could land a contract large enough to save her business while showing the people of New York what she was capable of before they found out who her father was and wrote her off.

Something that had happened one too many times, including when she'd first tried to find space for The Flower Bell. Her favorite spot, a corner shop close to her future sister-in-law's bookstore, had been her dream, one she'd scrimped and saved and kept her fingers crossed for, hoping it would come available around the time she was ready to launch.

By some miracle, it had been available. Until the leasing agent had found out who her father was and shared that her own father had lost his life savings investing in the Waldsworth Fund.

Alexandra brushed aside the hot rush of shame that pooled in her belly every time she remembered the agent's look of utter revulsion as she'd pointed to the door. She focused on the arrangement she'd brought with her and ran a critical eye over the flowers. Pamela's list of upcoming events for the Pearson Group included a brunch at the New York Public Library, a series of meals at a private address in the Hamptons and a formal reception at the Metropolitan Museum of Art.

"They're wining and dining prospective investors," Pamela had shared when they'd grabbed coffee last week, a tradition they'd carried on since they'd met in a community college class. "From what I hear, the client targets are the kind you'd see in Forbes. Whoever they are, the company's not holding back. They've gone with a mystery approach, only revealing a couple key contacts before they officially launch. Cloak and dagger, but it's working. Everyone's talking about them. The invitations they've sent out for their upcoming events are the most coveted in the city right now."

She'd decided to make a sample arrangement for the first event, the brunch. The low-lying design she'd created featured white roses and anise hyssop, tube-shaped clusters of lavender flowers, combined elegance with the soft color palettes of spring. Not too over-the-top that it would distract from the important business being conducted, but unique enough to generate conversation and show that Pearson could be both traditional and innovative.

She reached out and ran a finger over the velvet petal of a rose. The delicate, silky texture stirred a memory, one filled with the scents of violets and cedar entwined with amber. When she'd opened her eyes, nervous butterflies fluttering through her veins even as her body grew heavy with desire, it had been to see his face inches away, his full lips hovering over hers.

"Do you want this?" he'd asked, the growl in his voice betraying his desire. But still he'd held back, not wanting to hurt her, not wanting to push her.

And she'd loved him for that. She hadn't thought it possible to love him any more than she already did, but she'd fallen so deep in that moment that she'd given in to the sudden burst of confidence, leaned up and kissed him, her fingers tangling in his thick hair as she'd arched her naked hips against his.

She jerked her hand away from the rose. Eight and a half years. Nine in September. She usually did a better job keeping his memory at bay.

Maybe the roses were a bad idea.

Before she could do something foolish, like try to rearrange the flowers and toss the roses in the trash, the door to the conference room opened. The willow-thin woman in the black pencil skirt and red silk blouse, who had led her into the conference room, stood in the doorway. Silvery blond hair hung down her back, straightened and cut perfectly to frame her face. Alexandra nervously tucked a stray brown curl behind her ear. When the Waldsworths had been the Waldsworths of

Lower Manhattan, her father and his third wife, Susan, had pressured her to get her "plain brown hair" touched up with golden highlights to bring out her hazel eyes. Nowadays, getting anything more than a trim was beyond her budget.

But she should have splurged on a little more self-care before coming unannounced to a building like the Carlson and asking to speak with the events manager of the newly-formed Pearson Group. The company website had listed an official launch date two weeks from now, with interested parties encouraged to contact the CEO's executive assistant, Jessica Elliott. Fortunately, Pamela had been working with the Pearson Group's events manager, Laura Jones. It was easy to find Laura Jones, corporate event planner to the wealthiest companies in the Big Apple. Her feature in *Fortune* magazine and glossy images from past events she'd organized for other high-profile companies had shown an impeccably dressed woman with a stylish red bob, a brilliant white smile and a closet full of the latest couture.

Alexandra's throat tightened. She should have put more effort into her wardrobe, splurged on a name-brand outfit.

"The CEO will see you now."

Her heart skipped a beat. She swallowed past the baseball-size lump that suddenly rose in her throat.

"CEO?"

"Yes."

"What about Ms. Jones?"

Jessica's eyes narrowed slightly. "Have you spoken directly with Ms. Jones?"

No. After her emails, phone calls and attempts at booking in-person appointments with the other companies on Pamela's list, she'd decided to go all in on the Pearson Group and show up with an arrangement that would show Ms. Laura Jones what she was capable of. Better to make one final attempt and close her shop knowing she'd given it her all than to always wonder what if.

She just hadn't anticipated having to make her pitch to the mysterious CEO.

"I assumed with her being the events manager—"

"The majority of our staff are at a corporate training seminar in Shanghai this week."

Okay. She could handle this. Though why the CEO would have any interest in meeting with a struggling florist was beyond her. But instead of questioning her good fortune, she needed to grab the opportunity with both hands.

"All right. It's kind of him to make time for me."

A perfectly-tweezed eyebrow arched upward as something akin to amusement crossed Jessica's face. "It's not kindness. You piqued his interest."

"Hopefully in a good way."

A pale shoulder moved up and down in an elegant shrug. "That remains to be seen. He has five minutes." She glanced at her watch, silver and trimmed in diamonds judging by the way it glinted in the light. Probably Cartier. "Starting now, not a second more. Follow me, Miss Moss."

Steeling her spine, Alexandra tucked the portfolio under one arm, picked up the arrangement and followed the secretary out the door.

This is further than you've made it all week. Don't give up now.

The inner pep talk did little for the sudden light-headedness plaguing her as she tried to keep up with Jessica's rapid pace down a hall enclosed by glass, empty offices on one side and views of New York's impressive skyline on the other. How the woman managed to walk so quickly when she was sporting four-inch stilettos was beyond Alexandra. She could barely keep up in her plain black ballet flats.

Her nervousness reached a fever pitch as the secretary turned a corner and stopped in front of double mahogany doors polished to perfection. Was it possible for one's heart to beat so fast without passing out? The entire future of her company was riding on how she conducted herself in this meeting.

No pressure. None at all.

"He's waiting."

"Okay. Thank you. And his name?"

"He'll tell you."

Alexandra blinked. "What…"

Jessica gave her another look, one that was almost pitying, before she brushed past Alexandra and walked back down the hall, her heels clicking ominously against the floor as she disappeared around the corner.

Slowly, Alexandra turned back to the double doors. She'd met plenty of eccentric and egotistical millionaires in the twenty years she'd been known as Alexandra Waldsworth. The man waiting for her behind the double doors probably just enjoyed being the one in power.

The rational excuse didn't dispel the tension that tightened around her spine with a vise-like grip as she knocked on the doors.

"Enter."

The muffled voice, deep with the faintest of accents, wrapped around her. It almost sounded like...

Focus.

She pulled up the memory that had pushed her to succeed all these years: her father in his orange prison uniform glaring balefully at her from behind the glass of the visitor's booth. A moment later she'd stood and walked away as he'd hurled one final insult at her:

You'll never succeed. Not without me!

He'd thought to shred her confidence, to make her turn around and come crawling back. But it had done the opposite. It had released the shackles around her spirit, set her free as she'd walked away with the resolution to prove him wrong thundering in her veins.

That she had come to that realization a little over a year after she'd hurt the man she'd loved had come with its own pain, one that had faded over time but still kicked up every now and then.

Focus on the future. Focus on now.

She squared her shoulders and raised her chin. No matter what happened in the next five minutes, she could walk out with her head held high, knowing she'd tried.

She opened the door, a welcoming smile on her face.

"Good morning. Thank you for seeing me..."

Her voice trailed off as her steps faltered. She blinked several times, hoping against hope that she was just imagining things.

But the image stayed firm. A tall, broad-shouldered man dressed to perfection in a black Armani suit and red tie was seated behind one of the largest desks she'd ever seen. His face had hardened over the years, the lack of beard emphasizing the angular cut of his chin and the long, elegant line of his nose. His hair had been cut short on the sides and left longer on the top, swept to the side and styled so perfectly that not even a wisp dared to be out of place. He leaned back in his chair, his amber eyes sharp and focused on her with a cold intensity that made her feel like she was being examined under a microscope.

"Alexandra Waldsworth."

The rich timbre of his voice washed over her, sank beneath her skin and ignited a simmering warmth deep in her veins even though each syllable of her name was coated in icy disdain.

She glanced down, saw her business card sitting in the middle of the perfectly organized black walnut desk trimmed with glass edging. He must have looked her up, she realized as she tried to tamp down the nausea rising in the pit of her stomach.

Her eyes snapped back up to his and she barely kept her composure as she met his condescending stare. Why had he agreed to meet with her instead of having Jessica kick her out? Or even call the police to have her removed? Perhaps he had wanted to tell her to her face to never walk into the gleaming halls of the Pearson Group again.

"It's Moss now," she replied, proud that she managed to keep her voice steady.

He arched a brow. "Marry one of your rich beaus?"

"No. My mother's maiden name. I stopped going by Waldsworth years ago."

"Last I knew, you were dating some oil tycoon's son from Princeton." His lips curled into a sneer that nearly made her flinch. "Named after a car?"

"Royce."

She didn't elaborate. What was the point in explaining that her father had basically forced her to spend time in Royce's company in a bid to bring his parents on as investors in the Waldsworth Fund? That the one time Royce had attempted to kiss her, he'd reminded her more of an overexcited puppy than a potential lover?

"Didn't work out?"

"No." She gestured to the incredible view of the city's skyline. "You've done well for yourself, Grant. Congratulations."

"Mr. Santos," he corrected. "Chairman, CEO and founder of the Pearson Group." His eyes moved from her face to the flowers clutched in her hands. He raised one thick brow. "And you're now using a false name and selling flowers." One corner of his mouth flicked up. "My, my, how times have changed."

Guilt rooted her feet to the floor as the simmering warmth disappeared under a flush of hot shame. She deserved every bit of his contempt. He'd done nothing but love her, support her, encourage her. And when push had come to shove, she'd fallen beneath the force of her father's wrath instead of standing up for the man she loved.

The man who had obviously continued on to bigger and better things. Floor-to-ceiling windows to one side of the room gave yet another impressive view of Central Park and the cityscape. Behind Grant's desk black bookcases lined the walls, the shelves playing host to books on finance, politics and history, along with artfully-placed sculptures, awards and the occasional picture of Grant with people who looked very important. Leather chairs were arranged just so around a glass coffee table by the windows. Not what she would have pictured for Grant—too austere and cold—but that was based off the Grant Santos she'd known nine years ago.

"I apologize, Mr. Santos." How she managed to sound collected, she had no idea, but the sound of her own voice, quiet yet confident, gave her enough strength to meet his stare. "Had I known you were the head of the Pearson Group, I wouldn't have bothered you." She walked forward, acutely conscious of the material of her secondhand pants brushing against her legs as she moved to his desk and set the flower arrangement down, glass clinking on glass with a soft *tink* that sounded like a gunshot in the cavernous room. "Please accept this with my compliments and my apologies for taking your time. I'll see myself out."

She turned and walked away, as she'd done when she'd last seen him. Both times hot tears had burned at the backs of her eyes. Both times her heart felt like it was cracking in two. But this time she didn't want to turn around and throw herself into his arms. No, she just wanted to get as far away from him as possible.

Her hand was on the door handle when his voice rang out.

"You still have two minutes."

Her fingers tightened on the silver handle. It took every ounce of willpower to force herself to turn around and face him again.

"Excuse me?"

He gestured to the flower arrangement. "I told Miss Elliott you had five minutes. You still have two minutes to sell me on whatever it is you came here to pitch." Disdain flashed in his eyes as he glanced at the hyssop. "Perhaps you're looking for investment in a wildflower farm?"

Irritation steadied her feelings. The one constant in her life had been flowers. In the precious few years she'd had with her mother before she'd passed from cancer, Amelia Waldsworth had instilled a deep and abiding love of flowers in her daughter. From the native plants that grew in the woods around her mother's family home in upstate New York to creating bouquets filled with not just colorful blooms but also meaning, Alexandra's early life had been filled with flowers.

It had been one of the silver linings in the mess her father had created with his fraudulent dealings. A chance to start over, to move away from the corporate event-planning degree he'd bullied her into and instead pursue her true passion.

"You have a good eye, Mr. Santos. Those are lavender giant hyssop, a native wildflower found here in New York."

"And why have you brought me wildflowers?"

She steadied herself with a deep breath as she opened the leather portfolio, pulled out her proposal and laid it on his desk, resisting the temptation to take a giant step back. His tan fingers rested on the top page, but he didn't read it. His gaze stayed fixed on her face.

"You're courting new clients to sign on with the Pearson Group."

Not a flicker of emotion, not a single facial tic. The frozen expression, handsome as it was, made her unexpectedly sad. There had been a time when his face had shown her his every thought, from a joyful smile as he'd savored the simple pleasure of a glass of lemonade on a scorching summer's day to soul-wrenching heartbreak as she'd turned her back on him.

"What led you to that conclusion?"

"Rumor has it that you're hosting several events in two weeks' time, events to impress potential clients." She tapped the paper, making sure their fingers didn't touch. "I can help you do that."

"Aside from my curiosity about who would be so indiscreet as to share details of my private affairs, how will your collection of weeds help me convince clients with millions to billions of dollars to invest with the Pearson Group?"

"Flower arrangements at corporate events have been proven to increase guest perception of a space, the event they're attending and even the host themselves," she said, her voice firming as she warmed to the topic she'd pursued professionally. "Having fresh flowers can increase attendance, the attention span of your guests and demonstrate that you're investing in your prospective clients." She laid a gentle touch on a cluster of pale purple blossoms. "Given that you've recently moved here from Los Angeles, including a unique native flower along with the state flower of New York is a subtle but explicit gesture that you care about the small details, that you're not just moving here to make a quick buck before jetting off to your next destination."

"And you think the wealthiest of New York's residents will know the difference between a hyssop and a daffodil?"

"They will with the customized cards I include for events such as these that explain the meaning of the flowers in the arrangements."

Or they will, if you hire me, she added as she mentally crossed her fingers.

No one had yet given her the chance to make her grandest ideas come to life.

His eyes shifted to where her hand rested, his lips thinning. Her fingers trembled slightly as she removed her hand and let her arms fall to her sides, resisting the urge to cross them over her stomach.

"How long has your shop been open?"

"Six months."

He snorted. "What can you do that a more established shop can't?"

She pulled the proposal from beneath his fingers, taking care not to touch him, flipped the page and set it back in front of him. "I offer very competitive rates. I have five years of training with some of the top florists on the East Coast. And, most of all, I don't do the usual arrangements."

"Yes, I can see that."

Whether the words were meant as a compliment or an insult, she had no idea. And she didn't care, she realized with surprise and a small degree of pride. The arrangement was one of her best ones to date.

"The Flower Bell would be pleased to provide arrangements for your upcoming events, Mr. Santos. My phone number is on the card your secretary provided to you if you have any further questions."

Grant looked down at the paper and she took the opportunity to turn once more and head for the door. She'd tried and now her five minutes were more than up. He hadn't called security, hadn't yelled at her or called her names. Really, she consoled herself, it had gone better than she could have hoped for. At least she'd gotten good practice for the next time she made a pitch to a prospective client.

"Why should I hire you, Miss Waldsworth, after the way our last association ended?"

She nearly tripped over her own feet as her heartbeat stuttered. The question, she had no doubt, had been crafted to inflict as much pain as possible. But it was a fair one. She'd ruined his life once. Not that she had a snowball's chance in hell of him hiring her regardless, but she couldn't bear to hurt him again.

She turned and faced him the way she should have all those years ago.

"I'm good at my job, Mr. Santos. My business has excellent reviews. But I understand your concerns given the way things ended between us. If our previous history would impede what you're trying to accomplish, then I'm not the best choice. Thank you for your time."

She made it out the door and let it close behind her before he could say anything else. Her feet guided her down the hall, around the corner and to the elevator. Jessica was seated at a black desk, looking up to give a brief nod before resuming a phone call, allowing Alexandra to escape into the elevator.

The doors closed. The car whooshed down. Alexandra collapsed against the wall, keeping her gaze averted from the mirrors surrounding her and the chandelier gently swinging overhead. She bit down on her lower lip, the tiny burst of pain enabling her to keep her sorrow locked in her chest.

Of all the people to agree to hear her pitch, it had to be Grant Santos. The first, and only, man she'd ever given herself to. The one man she'd loved, and who had loved her in turn, until she'd been so weak and allowed her father to ruin their chances at a happily-ever-after.

The man who had fathered her child, a child she'd found out about and lost just weeks after she'd cut Grant from her life.

She scrunched her eyes shut, willed herself to stand straight as the elevator neared the first floor. If she'd entertained any possibilities of Grant booking The Flower Bell, those hopes had been dashed by his razor-sharp query.

As she walked out of the Carlson and halfheartedly raised an arm to flag down a taxi, she wondered not for the first time if she'd made a mistake pursuing her career in New York. Perhaps she should have moved out of the city, or even to a new state.

It seemed no matter how fast she ran, her past would always be one step behind her.

CHAPTER TWO

GRANT SANTOS WATCHED Alexandra Waldsworth, or Moss or whatever the hell she was calling herself these days, walk through the reception area on the security screen. She returned Jessica's nod before stepping into the elevator. As the doors swished shut, Alexandra stared straight ahead, her hands clenched around the leather portfolio in her hands as if it was a lifeline.

How was it possible for him to feel anything approaching sympathy for the woman who'd broken his heart and orchestrated his firing all those years ago? Yet, it was most definitely sympathy that tugged at his chest as he looked down at the proposal in front of him.

She'd come down quite a bit in the world since he'd last seen her nine years ago. She'd looked good—*too good*—in an ivory tie-neck blouse and emerald green pants that followed the long curve of her legs. But he hadn't missed the subtle signs that Alexandra was no longer shopping at Chanel or Saint Laurent: the scuff marks on her shoes, the slight fraying at the end of one of the ties on her blouse and the lack of highlights in her dark brown hair. A far cry from the polished socialite he'd fallen in love with.

She'd looked like a sun-kissed mermaid when he'd

first laid eyes on her all those years ago, white teeth brilliant against perfectly tanned skin as she'd laughed up at him when he'd asked if she was one of the gardeners. A reasonable assumption, she'd assured him as he'd helped her to her feet, since she'd been sitting on the grass pulling weeds. It had been two days of walks in the gardens and long, intimate conversations before she'd revealed her name and that her father was the one who'd hired him as a seasonal landscaper. By then, it was too late. He was entranced.

Perhaps if she'd told him who she was that first day, he never would have allowed himself to fall for her. Never would have been duped by the illusion she'd created.

He pressed a button beneath his desk.

"Is the report ready, Jessica?"

"Yes, sir. Emailing it now."

"Give me five minutes, then report to my office."

"Yes, sir."

As he waited for the email from his preferred security company to arrive, he clicked on the website he'd minimized when he'd heard the clicking of Jessica's absurdly tall stilettos outside his office, signaling the arrival of his unexpected guest. The *About Us* page of The Flower Bell's website featured a photo of Alexandra in a plain yellow shirt and blue jeans, her face lit up as if the photographer had captured her midlaugh. She was holding up a terra-cotta pot overflowing with some bushy white flower.

When Jessica had walked in and handed him a business card for The Flower Bell, he'd noted the name of the proprietor. He'd been annoyed at the interruption to his carefully planned day. Still, he'd typed in the website address, intrigued as to who would have the guts to show up without an appointment.

Even though his office was on the forty-sixth floor, he'd initially chalked up the dull roaring in his ears to the sounds of New York traffic when Alexandra's smile had filled his computer screen. It had taken a moment for him to realize it was the pounding of blood rushing through his body as his heart sped up at the sight of his former lover. After that last photo of her with her new beau, he hadn't seen her in years. And it wasn't just being confronted with her image. No, it was that she looked so happy. Not the false smile he'd seen her paste on her face when she'd made the rounds at one of her father's summer parties, but the kind of wide grin that made her hazel eyes crinkle at the corners.

He'd once been the source of that smile. But, he'd reminded himself bitterly as he'd scrolled through the website, it had been an act. Alexandra was an excellent actress. What game was she playing now by suddenly showing up at his office after all these years? She'd finagled not only the name of his events manager, but also the list of exclusive events Laura had put together to entice his executive team's most-wanted prospective clients. Whatever she was up to, she had already shown herself to still be cunning and manipulative. Never in his wildest dreams would he have guessed that Alexandra Moss, owner of a little floral shop on the outskirts of SoHo, had any connection to his past.

Although, if he'd been linked to a man as sadistic and greedy as her father, he probably would have changed his name, too. David Waldsworth had been convicted of multiple crimes, including witness intimidation, during his trial. Grant had known the bare basics. It had been impossible to avoid the twenty-four-seven news coverage. It had been a wonderful spring day as he'd watched the verdict delivered: guilty on all accounts, with a prison sentence that ensured David Waldsworth would die in jail.

Grant had toasted the jury with a beer in a café on the Santa Monica pier and then turned from the TV to order another round before the camera could pan over the people seated in the courtroom. Whether Alexandra had been there or not, he didn't care to see her face, see whether she cried fat crocodile tears for the man she'd let witness his humiliation. Instead, he'd focused on the deep satisfaction of watching a man known for his cruelties finally get his comeuppance.

But he hadn't completely been able to disconnect from the Waldsworth name or legacy. It had been a frequent topic in many of his early graduate courses. Fortunately, the coverage had focused on David, his firm, the victims of his crimes and the new laws that had been enacted in the wake of the trial. Very little was mentioned of David's family. Anytime Grant had even the tiniest bit of temptation to look Alexandra up, he squashed it with a ruthlessness he'd developed in the months after their breakup.

She was a part of his past. Never to be a part of his present or future again.

Until she'd literally walked back into his life with her fake, wide-eyed innocence and her carefully-curated appearance of a down-on-her-luck businesswoman.

His lips curled into a scowl as he scanned The Flower Bell's website. Once he'd realized who Alexandra Moss truly was, he'd had Jessica place her in the conference room as he'd conducted a quick review online while tasking his security company with digging into the past nine years of her life. Her business appeared legitimate and, given that she had started it a month before he'd decided to move back to New York, hadn't been created for the sake of trapping him into some scheme.

Unfortunately, he'd found precious little beyond her website, an Instagram page for the shop and old news articles about the Waldsworth Fund scandal. Still, satisfaction had settled deep into his bones as he'd consumed several of the articles on the fall of the high and mighty David Waldsworth. All of his homes, including the Hamptons beach house, had been sold by the U.S. Marshals to compensate his victims. David's wife, Susan, had filed for divorce and been allowed to keep half a million dollars. A fortune to many but, from what Grant remembered of Susan and her preference for all things name brand, probably not enough to keep her lifestyle funded for even a year.

As to David's daughter and stepson, Finley—a spoiled brat who had made Alexandra's life hell—there was hardly any mention of them. The majority of the news coverage had focused on David and his unapologetic interviews from prison.

Alexandra.

The first month after she'd looked at him, her lip curled in disgust, and denounced him in front of her father, he'd dreamed of her every night. He'd replayed their every encounter, from the first time he'd seen her in the gardens of the Waldsworth mansion in the Hamptons to the night they'd first kissed atop the Ferris wheel at a carnival, the roar of the ocean a background to the thundering of his heart as he'd tasted honey on her lips and surrendered himself to the fact that he'd fallen in love. None of it had made sense. He knew without a doubt he'd been Alexandra's first lover. What had happened between the night they'd made love on the beach and the very next day when she'd broken things off?

Even though it had been so long ago, humiliation still burned a slow, painful trail in his gut. He loathed admitting that he'd hoped something would change, that she would reach out and tell him it had all been a horrible mistake. It hadn't been until he'd seen a picture of Alexandra circulating on Instagram, smiling up at some blond Ivy League-looking trust fund brat, with the date showing it had been taken at her family's weekend party the day after she'd broken his heart, that he'd fully accepted he had been exactly what she'd told him—a summer fling, nothing more.

You're just a gardener, Grant. I'm a Waldsworth. It's been fun, but it was never going to last.

Since that photo had been published—and he'd barely resisted the urge to track down the man who dared to have his arm around Alexandra's waist and threaten him within an inch of his life—he'd purged everything that reminded him of her. He'd thrown himself into his studies and, been accepted into Stanford University's graduate business program for the spring semester. Since the day the plane had taken off from the airport and carried him to the Golden Coast the week before Christmas, he'd allowed himself to think about Alexandra exactly once a year, on Labor Day weekend when he raised a glass of scotch to her and her father. As painful as it had been, he had them to thank for his current success.

Her betrayal had also allowed him to focus on other more important goals. Goals like achieving a level of wealth that would ensure he and his mother never experienced poverty again. Goals like avenging his father and opening the door for a return to his country.

And now the goal of becoming what David and Alexandra Waldsworth hadn't believed him capable of—one of the denizens of New York's elite.

His computer beeped. With a couple taps on the keyboard, the initial background review of one Alexandra Moss, née Waldsworth, was pulled up on his screen. Wayne Security had demonstrated once again why they deserved the outrageous retainer he paid them every year with an initial detailed ten-page report and a guarantee from its president, Joseph, that a full write-up would be delivered by midnight. The Flower Bell was indeed a licensed and insured business, although one that was barely scraping by. Alexandra was financially stretched to the breaking point, and that was with a business address in a rundown part of town and her personal address listed as a one-room flat behind a bookstore nearby. The rest of the report carried meager but telling details: her spotty employment history with various florists while working gig jobs like waitressing or walking dogs, her graduation from a community college instead of Princeton.

Yes, Alexandra was definitely in trouble.

He looked down at the cream-colored papers in his hand, complete with a silver bell wrapped in flowers at the top. None of the possibilities of why Alexandra had chosen now to reenter his life had included her pitching her business for his upcoming Pearson Group client recruitment events.

Crawling back after discovering his wealth and status, maybe. Or some other nefarious scheme. But running a small business that was on the verge of collapsing? That possibility hadn't been anywhere on his radar.

Anger stiffened the muscles in his neck. Did she really think he'd bail her out? It also brought up the question of how she'd found out what he and his executives were planning. He'd have to find out who talked. The mystery approach of generating interest in the Pearson Group had not been his first choice. But he had to give credit to the team he'd so meticulously put together. The enigmatic tactics, from select potential clients being sent invitations and a fifty-page packet on the investment options, corporate backgrounds of Pearson's team and plans for the future, had netted him nearly one hundred of New York's wealthiest residents for the brunch at the New York Public Library, with the five richest families also joining him for a week at his Hamptons house.

A house he had purchased partially for the incredible ocean view and private beach, and partially because it rivaled the home just a couple miles away where he had experienced the most intense pleasure and pain he'd ever known.

He dropped Alexandra's proposal on his desk and glanced around the office with a critical eye. Three of the walls had been painted a grayish navy, sedate and refined, a pleasing backdrop for the mix of modern, geometric silver light fixtures and brown leather chairs seated in front of his desk.

His entire body had tightened when Alexandra had approached his desk, shoulders thrown back with confidence, hazel eyes glinting with determination. She'd had every reason to appear guilty, embarrassed, humiliated. Instead, she'd stood in front of him and delivered a surprisingly articulate and convincing argument for doing the flowers for his events.

He'd need to look into who had been so indiscreet as to let the details of those events slip. But, he acknowledged as he picked up the proposal again, Alexandra had certainly done her homework. Her prices were competitive, even cheap, her knowledge of flowers and the floral industry evident in the details she'd included in her write-up.

Not surprising, he thought with a reluctant twinge of admiration. He could still remember the first time he'd seen her: golden brown hair tucked under a straw hat; the curves of her young body clad in a bright yellow tank top and jean shorts as she'd pulled weeds from the base of a rose plant along one of the winding paths in the gardens. When she'd glanced at him over her shoulder with that sunny, sweet smile, he'd been lost.

But not anymore, he sternly reminded himself as he tossed the paper on his desk and stood, hardening his heart to the happy memories.

Memories and fairy tales, he thought as he moved to the glass wall of his office with purposeful strides and gazed down at the bustling streets of New York City. *Aside from the incredible sex, none of it was real.*

No, he'd made real progress after he'd accepted that Alexandra had used and discarded him. He'd graduated with his master's degree in business, accrued his first million before he was thirty and now stood on the cusp of becoming a billionaire before he was thirty-five. If he played his cards right, the Pearson Group would become one of the premier investment firms on the East Coast.

He turned back toward his desk, the unique arrangement catching his eye. It was striking, and despite the person behind the proposal, she'd made a good pitch.

That he had the upper hand this time certainly didn't hurt. In fact, he thought as he turned the possibility around in his mind, hiring Alexandra would serve two purposes. Adding a little extra class to the upcoming events, yes, but also showing her exactly what she had thrown away. He smiled as the plan formed, solidified in his mind. It would be even more satisfying to have the once high and mighty Alexandra Waldsworth working for him, following his every order as he wined and dined the kind of people she'd once shared dinners with. She had the gall to come to him for help after what she'd done to him—used him as her personal toy while whispering false words of love in response to his sharing a piece of his soul—so turnabout was fair play. While she struggled to maintain employment and make a go of what seemed like a rich girl's fantasy, he would show her up close and personally everything he had achieved, from his multimillion-dollar firm to the numerous luxuries his money could now buy.

Not bad for *just a gardener.*

He hit the button for Jessica's line.

"Yes, Mr. Santos?"

"Reach out to Laura Jones and ask her to get three proposals for flowers for the upcoming events. Something similar to the proposal Miss Waldsworth left us."

"Waldsworth, sir?"

"Miss Moss," Grant corrected with gritted teeth. "I want the proposals by five p.m."

"Yes, sir."

He tapped a finger against the papers on his desk, his

lips tilting up. This time he wouldn't give Alexandra a single chance to hurt him again. From here on out, he would be in control.

CHAPTER THREE

ALEXANDRA STARED MOROSELY into her glass of red wine. The relaxing strains of jazz played against a backdrop of clinking glasses and hushed voices as customers milled around the shelves of The Story Keeper. A gentle spring rain tapped against the window. New Yorkers rushed by outside, umbrellas shielding their faces from the prying eyes of shoppers and diners ensconced in the warm interiors of the stores and restaurants lining one of Greenwich Village's popular streets.

"What's eating you?"

Alexandra took a long sip of wine as her stepbrother, Finn, dropped into the seat across from her. Hard to imagine the boy who ignored her existence as a teenager, unless he was mercilessly teasing her or ordering her about, had become her closest friend. Or that he would fall in love with a bookshop manager instead of a wealthy socialite.

Normally, she loved savoring a glass of red and flipping through a mystery book at her future sister-in-law's bookstore. That it was a darkening, rainy evening should have made it perfect.

But instead of vivid images of a plucky heroine tracking a potential murderer through the streets of

London filling her mind, all she saw was Grant. Grant's eyes, so cold as he stared at her with disdain. Grant's lips, twisted into that menacing smirk. Grant's shoulders, broader and more muscular than the last time he'd held her against him and whispered romantic sentiments in Portuguese.

Had she really believed she'd placed all that behind her? Because right now it hurt just as much, if not more, than the day she'd laughed in his face and told him she'd never date a common gardener, much less fall in love with one.

Yup, she thought as she took another, longer, sip. *I deserve every bit of his contempt. Didn't mean a single word, but how was he supposed to know that?*

"Nothing."

Finn reached across the table and placed his hand over the top of her glass.

"If your goal is to get drunk, Amanda just got a port in. I hate wine, but even I drink that stuff."

An unwilling smile tugged at her lips. It was hard to picture the man sitting across from her, dressed in jeans and a black T-shirt with a little white book stitched on the pocket, as the former Finley Waldsworth, Princeton graduate, womanizer, rising star at Waldsworth Financial and favored by her father so much that he'd formally adopted his stepson so that he would "have a son with the Waldsworth name."

Now he was just plain Finn Davids, an economics teacher at a local high school, and engaged to the manager of a bookstore and adjoining coffee shop.

Finn's teasing smile disappeared as his hand shifted off her glass and settled on her wrist.

"Amanda and I can loan you some money, Alex."

Alexandra shook her head.

"Absolutely not. You have a wedding coming up, a house to buy and I expect by this time next year a nursery to fill."

Did it make her a rotten sister that her heart twisted with a slight pang of envy as Finn's eyes automatically warmed and slid to the blonde woman behind the cash register? Amanda caught his appreciative gaze and blew him a kiss before throwing Alexandra a wink. Alexandra raised her wineglass toward the woman who had brought her stepbrother to his knees two years ago.

"What about your plan to pitch The Flower Bell's services to some of Pamela's clients?"

"I actually made it into the office of one of them today."

Finn perked up. "Oh?"

Amanda walked up to their table and set a small-bowled glass filled with a dark ruby liquid in front of Finn and a fruit and cheese plate in front of Alexandra.

"Did you get a contract?" Amanda asked excitedly as she slid into the chair next to Finn. Finn looped an arm around his fiancée's shoulders.

"Not exactly." She swirled the remaining wine in her glass and tossed back the rest of it. "It was Grant Santos."

Finn choked on his port and Amanda reached over and plucked the glass from his hand before he spilled the rest on the table.

"Grant?" Finn managed to finally gasp. "What's he doing in New York?"

"Who's Grant?" Amanda asked.

Alexandra shot her stepbrother a pleading look. She loved Amanda and considered her a good friend, but just the thought of explaining her tumultuous history with Grant made her want to crawl under the covers of her bed and sleep for a week.

"Grant was Alexandra's...boyfriend," Finn finally said. "My stepfather made them split up after a summer romance when she was nineteen."

Amanda's usually sunny expression darkened. She despised David Waldsworth. David had been fixated on Finn's success. Even though Finn had been Susan's son from her first marriage, he had become the son he'd never had. He hadn't accepted Finn's change of heart, his preference for a simpler life. He had written to his stepson numerous times encouraging Finn to dump Amanda and hold out for a woman who could return him to the lifestyle he'd been raised in. That Finn and Amanda were genuinely happy made no difference.

"Bastard."

"Agreed."

Alexandra stared glumly at her empty wineglass.

"I'll get you another," Amanda said, standing before Alexandra could protest. She leaned down, gave Alexandra a sisterly hug and disappeared into the back.

"You're really lucky, Finn."

"I am," her stepbrother agreed, "but don't try to change the subject. What happened?"

"He's doing well for himself." *Very well.* "Starting a new investment firm here in New York City. The Pearson Group."

Finn let out a low whistle. "I've heard about them. Grant's heading it?"

"Yeah. CEO and a couple other titles." She smiled slightly. "He's achieved a lot."

"Apparently. Did he book The Flower Bell? Was he nice to you?"

"No, and…coldly polite would be a better way to describe it."

Finn frowned. "If he knew what you went through—"

"He doesn't, and he's not going to," Alexandra said firmly. "There's no point in rehashing the past. I made my choice and I have to live with it. I let Father tell me what to do. I said horrible, awful things and I got him fired."

"He threatened to deport Grant and his mother if you kept seeing him," Finn retorted. "And then you got preg—"

"Finn!"

Finn stopped midsentence, eyes narrowed, a vein ticking in his forehead. Finn was the only one besides the doctor and nurses in the emergency room who knew what had happened that awful October night. He'd been the one to rush her to the hospital when, after a few weeks of feeling exhausted, she'd suddenly started to bleed as a sharp pain stabbed her abdomen. He'd held her hand as the doctor had delivered the horrifying news; that she was pregnant with Grant's baby and was in the middle of miscarrying. He'd stayed with her at the hospital, cared for her at home and covered for her when she'd been bedridden the following week when David and Susan had come back from one of their frequent luxury vacations.

It had been the second of the two worst moments of her life. But if there were silver linings to be found, she could identify her tragedy as the turning point in her relationship with her stepbrother. They'd grown closer. Finn had matured almost overnight. When their worlds came crashing down just a couple months later, they'd had each other.

"I didn't know Grant well," Finn finally said. "But he seemed like a rational guy. And I do think he really cared for you, Alex." He reached out again and squeezed her hand. "You could still tell him what happened."

Not what I need to hear right now.

"No, Finn. Chances are I'll never see Grant Santos again."

"Good evening, Miss Waldsworth."

The dark voice cut through the pleasant din of the bookshop. Alexandra closed her eyes, willing the deep, rich tones that wrapped around her with the familiarity of a lover's caress to be a figment of her imagination.

"My apologies for interrupting your date."

Her eyes flew open at the whiplike lash of words. She turned in her chair to see Grant Santos in all his handsome glory standing just a couple feet behind her chair. He'd changed out of the custom-tailored suit. Even in a more casual outfit of dark blue jeans and a cream-colored sweater stretched perfectly over his large shoulders, sleeves rolled up to his elbows, he exuded wealth and sophistication from the silver Rolex glinting on his wrist to the dark gray Barbour raincoat draped over one arm.

"Grant." She mentally kicked herself. "Mr. Santos. What are you doing here?"

Grant's brown eyes flicked from her face down to where Finn's hand still rested on top of hers.

"I'm following up on your business proposal. It seems I've come at a bad time."

Finn stood and held out his hand.

"Long time, no see, Grant."

Grant's thick eyebrows drew together before recognition dawned on his face. Alexandra bit back a smile as his lips parted, the only sign of surprise. Grant glanced down at Finn's outstretched hand and let it hang in the air for a moment before shaking it.

"I didn't recognize you, Finley."

"Not having a stick shoved so far up where the sun doesn't shine probably helps."

Grant didn't even crack a smile.

"Yes."

Finn chuckled. "Still a straight shooter."

An elderly woman with fluffy white hair and hunched shoulders walked up to them.

"Excuse me, young man, do you work here? I saw your shirt, and I need your help looking for a romance book."

"Happy to help." Finn nodded to Grant. "Be nice to my sister."

Grant didn't respond, merely watched as Finn offered the customer his arm and escorted her toward a group of floor-to-ceiling shelves near the back. Alexandra took advantage of his moment of distraction to take in the details she'd missed earlier: the threads of silver in his thick black hair; the slight shadowing of whiskers along his sculpted jaw; the confidence he'd grown into since she'd last seen him, no longer cocky but self-assured in who he was and what he had accomplished.

Her heart twisted and she wrenched her gaze away. Where would they be if she'd trusted him with the truth? If she hadn't let her own fears overcome her love for him? If she'd stood up to her father?

That last thought sent a fresh wave of shame washing over her and she looked down at her replenished wineglass. Losing Grant had been the highest price she'd paid for her own weakness. But she'd let her father order her about for pretty much her whole life, from her clothes to her college degree. Even when she'd heard the first murmurings of something not being right at Waldsworth Investments, of dollars not adding up, she'd cowered before her father's anger when she'd summoned enough nerve to confront him. And then she'd let it go until the police had arrested him at a company holiday party the Christmas after she'd broken things off with Grant.

Most days she felt like she'd paid her dues, living paycheck to paycheck, making donations to several charities she knew had supported her father's victims, forgoing luxuries like dinner at a Michelin-starred restaurant.

Yet, on days like today, she wondered if she'd ever pay the price for the people she'd hurt.

Awareness danced across her skin. Steeling herself, she looked up and met Grant's amber gaze. Her breath caught in her chest. Once he'd looked at her as if he couldn't believe she was real, as if she was the most precious thing in the world to him. For a moment she thought she saw a flicker of that old heat.

But no, she must have imagined it, because the coldness in his eyes could have frozen fire.

"This doesn't seem like your kind of place," she finally said.

"Yours, either. And certainly not your stepbrother's," Grant replied as he sat in Finn's vacant seat, his gaze roaming over the worn but colorful armchairs and sofas scattered among the towering bookshelves, then toward the back of the shop where two double glass doors led out to the little patio Finn had renovated for Amanda. Café lights lit up the wet paving stones. It was empty for now, but Finn would soon move the mismatched wrought-iron tables and chairs out of storage for the warmer seasons. Amanda and Alexandra would plant flowers, and the space would be transformed into an outdoor eating space and small venue for local musicians.

Definitely not the luxury shops and high-end restaurants she had frequented with David and his wives and girlfriends over the years. She could only imagine how many experiences she'd missed out on by falling in line with her father's snobbery.

"How did you find me?"

"I went to your shop. It was closed, so my security firm looked up your home address. I saw you through the window when my limo pulled up." He cast another dubious look toward the shelves where Finn had disappeared. "How did Finn come to own a bookstore?"

"His fiancée's family owns it and she's the manager. Finn helps out when he's not teaching."

"I never would have imagined Finley Waldsworth engaged to a retail manager. Or teaching," Grant added dryly.

"It's Finn Davids now. He went back to his birth father's name. And he and Amanda are very happy."

Grant watched her for a long moment.

"Are you happy, Alexandra?"

She covered her surprise by reaching for her wineglass, all too conscious of his opaque gaze focused squarely on her.

"I am," she finally replied.

The cynical twist of his lips told her he saw right through her bold-faced lie.

"Disappointed with your new station in life?"

She frowned and set her glass down a little more forcefully than she intended, the wine nearly sloshing over the rim.

"Do you think I'm that big of a snob?"

"'I would rather die than be seen in public with a gardener.'"

Her stomach dropped as the words she'd fired at him all those years ago hit her in the chest. She'd said terrible, cruel things as she'd watched her father out of the corner of her eye. The more pleased he'd looked, the nastier she'd become, hoping that she was putting on enough of the performance he wanted that he would leave Grant and his mother alone.

Whether David would have gone after Grant and his mother later out of sheer spite would never be known, as just four months later he'd been arrested.

"I was a different person back then."

"Clearly."

She closed her eyes for a moment, trying to summon what little strength she had before giving up. What did it matter if Grant saw her as she was feeling tonight—defeated, lonely and on the verge of giving up? He loathed her. She didn't need to try and impress him. She would never get back in his good graces.

"I'm sorry, Grant. I hurt you."

He stared at her for a long moment.

"You did."

Not a hint of inflection in his deep, accented voice.

"I know." *I did it because I loved you.* "It might be hard to believe, but I am happy for you. I'm struggling right now with my business, but—" she waved a hand around at the shelves stacked with books "—personally, I'm the happiest I've ever been. That's more than a lot of people have." She forced a small smile. "Eventually, my head will catch up to my heart and I'll focus more on the blessings I do have." She started to stand. "But right now, unless you have something else to say, I'm going to say good-night. I have a busy day tomorrow and—"

"The Pearson Group would like to hire The Flower Bell."

CHAPTER FOUR

GRANT WATCHED AS Alexandra slowly sat back in her chair, her eyes wide with shock. He silently cursed. He'd planned on going about things very differently tonight, coming in more aggressively. But when she'd started to leave, unwanted sympathy and a hint of apprehension had pushed the words out of his mouth.

He'd spent the past nine years singularly focused on his career. Emotions like anger and jealousy had no place in his life. The two relationships he'd had over the years had been pleasant enough. He'd ended his time with Michelle, an accountant for a film production firm, when she'd started hinting at her favorite cut of diamond. Lindsay, a wildlife photographer, had texted him from Madagascar to apologize. She'd met someone and she hadn't seen him in three months anyway, so hopefully he wasn't too put out.

He'd written a brief text that had gone beyond his initial thoughts of *not put out at all*.

So when he'd walked into the bookstore and seen a dark-haired man with his hand covering Alexandra's, the jealousy that had unfurled in his chest and roared with a primal howl had been unexpected.

Unexpected and very much unwanted.

Even if he had wanted to rekindle his romance with Alexandra—which he reminded himself very sternly he did not—he would never be able to trust her. Not after the abrupt about-face, the vile words she'd hurled at him, getting him fired and to top it all off, dating Mr. Named-After-a-Car the day after their breakup.

But when he'd seen her there, looking so sad and being comforted by another man, he'd wanted to toss her over his shoulder, stalk out in the rain to the nearest cab, throw her in and take her back to his place to demand all the answers he'd never received before kissing her senseless.

Suspicion whispered across the back of his neck. Despite the red haze of fury coating his gaze when he'd seen the photos on Instagram of her and Royce, there had been something about her posture, a strain in her smile, that had seemed off.

He gave himself a mental shake. All these years and he was still searching for answers when the truth was right in front of him. Alexandra had been a rich, spoiled brat who had used him for a fling, and with the summer drawing to a close, had chosen to return to her life of luxury.

"You want to hire me?"

He scowled. He'd expected a little more gratitude, even a relieved smile, not misgivings. He'd had his driver go by her shop first, then her home address when they'd passed by the dark windows of The Flower Bell. He'd wanted to deliver the news in person, savor her gratefulness in her rundown store or her tiny little apartment situated behind a string of shops, let her meager environment punctuate the generosity of his offer.

And instead, he'd nearly lost his iron grip on his emotions and was now prodding her to accept.

"Yes."

"Why?"

He tamped down his irritation so he didn't overplay his hand.

"Your proposal was strong and your arrangement unique. Our event planner, Laura Jones, reached out to three of her florist contacts for competitive bids. One didn't deliver by the deadline, one submitted ideas I could find in a grocery store and the third, while unique, listed a price triple that of yours. Ms. Jones was impressed by your work, as was I."

A sentiment he meant, even if his offer of employment came with ulterior motives. He wouldn't make a job offer if she didn't have something to offer him in return. Revenge alone was not worth risking everything he had poured into his company.

Alexandra's lips parted. His eyes darted down, then swept back up to meet her gaze.

"I can't believe Ms. Jones picked me."

The awed innocence in her voice made his blood boil. The woman belonged on Broadway. She'd seduced him with the same wide-eyed, naive act. Not only would he not be fooled again, but this time when their association came to an end, she would be the one left with regrets.

He tamped down his anger and smoothed his face into a cold mask as he started to stand.

"If you're not confident in your own abilities, Miss Moss, then perhaps this wasn't a good idea."

"Wait!"

He suppressed a smile that his bluff had worked so quickly. Slowly, he sat back down.

"I'm just… You have to admit, given our history, it's not unreasonable to wonder why you'd want to work with me."

"You and your father taught me a valuable lesson all those years ago. I've become adept at removing emotion from business." He ignored her flinch, even as something shifted in his chest at the low blow. "You presented a detailed proposal with very competitive rates. My events manager conducted additional research and agreed with my initial impression. You were the best choice."

She blew out a slow breath.

"Okay."

"Okay?"

She shook her head slightly, dark brown hair tumbling down over one shoulder. Once upon a time he'd run his hands through her hair, savoring the feeling of silk gliding over his skin as he'd kissed every inch of her.

He threaded his fingers together on top of the table. It had been nearly a year since he'd seen Lindsay, the last time he'd had sex. He and Alexandra had a history. It was only natural for his body to respond to pleasant memories.

Pleasant? a vicious inner voice cackled. *What about the most intense, physically and emotionally satisfying lovemaking you've ever—*

"I'm sorry, Gra— Mr. Santos." She smiled, and damn his heart if it didn't lift a little at seeing the genuine hope on her face. "It's been a trying few weeks. I think I'm in shock, but I appreciate you accepting my proposal and am looking forward to working for the Pearson Group."

She held out her hand. He eyed it for a moment before steeling himself and returning the gesture. If he was going to live up to what he had said, that he could keep business separate from their tumultuous past, he needed to not be afraid of something as simple as a handshake.

Except there was nothing simple about feeling her warm skin against his again as his hand grasped hers. The hint of callouses on her palms from working with the plants; the warmth emanating from her skin made more potent after coming in from the cool spring storm; the softness in her smile. All of it melded together into a siren's song that lured him back into the past.

No.

He released her hand and pulled his phone out, focusing his attention on the screen and off the quickened tempo of his heartbeat.

"I'm notifying Jessica to schedule an appointment with you to go over the events, their locations and what we're looking for. Even though your mole provided some detail, I would prefer you get any further details from me."

He shot her a look he'd perfected at Stanford, one he'd learned from a grizzly finance professor who had made undergraduates to corporate financiers quake. But if Alexandra felt intimidated or pressured into revealing her source, she certainly didn't show it as she calmly returned his stare.

At least she had loyalty to someone. He would pursue that line of inquiry later, use it as leverage if needed.

"Aren't you the CEO and some other fancy titles?"

"Yes."

"So why won't I be working with Ms. Jones?"

"You will some. But with the team in Shanghai until two days before the first event, your primary contacts will be myself and my executive assistant, Jessica."

Something dark and sad flashed in Alexandra's eyes.

"And you don't trust me."

The words were uttered so softly they were nearly buried beneath the murmured conversations, music and clinks of glasses and cups. If he hadn't experienced firsthand how she could make love as if her soul had been on fire for him and less than twenty-four hours later deliver the cruelest, most vicious insults as she sent him packing, he would almost believe her act.

"No. I don't trust you."

To her credit, she didn't tear up, didn't make excuses. She simply nodded.

"Okay."

It would have been easier, less painful, if she had protested, if she'd descended into hysterics. But both of them simply acknowledging the truth stole some of his determination and replaced it with an ache for what had been.

Or at least what he thought had been.

"Now that we understand each other, I'll be adding a fifty percent completion bonus to the contract if everything is done satisfactorily."

He'd intended the offer as a demonstration that at this point in his life money truly didn't matter. He would achieve his first billion before the year was out with his own personal investments, and that wasn't including whether or not the Pearson Group took off the way he wanted. But when her eyes lit up with gratitude, his initial flare of smug satisfaction flamed out as quickly as it had appeared, replaced by something almost like guilt.

Mercilessly, he pushed that feeling aside. She was getting paid, and generously. If she delivered, she would have more than enough business to keep her little shop from going under. And, he reminded himself again, when it came to emotions, she was manipulative and heartless. Giving her a taste of her own medicine as he helped save her business was nothing to feel guilty over. He had more than earned the right to enjoy this feeling of power.

"That's not necessary."

"It's not," he agreed, "but Jessica wrote it into the contract."

Her smile grew. "I can't thank you enough, Mr. Santos." She pulled out her own phone and started tapping away. "Do you have time for a couple questions?"

"Jessica will provide you with all the information you need."

A frown furrowed her brow. "Which is great. But these are clients you're courting, right? It would be helpful to hear what you're thinking firsthand."

A professional answer, and one that made sense. So why was he resisting? Why did he suddenly feel the need to put as much distance between himself and Alexandra Moss as possible?

"I have ten minutes."

The quick flash of another smile pricked his skin.

"Ten minutes. All right, first question…"

He answered her inquiries deftly, savored the surprise in her eyes as he listed some of the guests who would be in attendance at the brunch, the house party and the final gala. Big names and even bigger wallets.

"I can't believe you got Theodore Craig to come," she said. "He's notoriously private. In all the summers we visited the Hamptons, I think I saw him once."

"I worked for him after you fired me."

The color disappeared from her face. "Oh."

"Started off as just mowing lawns. He invited me to have coffee with him one morning. When he learned I was studying finance, we started talking." The memory warmed him, steadied him. It hadn't just been his heart that had taken a fatal blow that Labor Day weekend. His confidence had been ripped asunder, too. Had he been deluding himself that he could achieve the goals he'd set for himself?

It had been Theodore who had looked at him not just with interest but respect, who had listened to his opinions on current events and economics and guided him toward applying for Stanford's graduate program. Who, Grant had found out when he'd graduated, had paid for it.

Theodore, a millionaire several hundred times over, had treated him like an equal. Unlike David, who had treated him like scum, and Alexandra, who had used him for her own amusement.

Alexandra glanced at her watch and grimaced.

"Sorry. I took twelve minutes."

"You had good questions."

Ridiculous that such a simple compliment warmed her.

"Thank you. And I got your invite to meet with Jessica tomorrow to tour the library and see the space the first luncheon is being held at."

Even though working with her ex-lover was not her

first choice, she couldn't deny the excitement and sense of purpose that had taken her from despondent to energized and determined. She enjoyed filling the small orders, a bouquet for a proposal or an arrangement to congratulate someone on a new career. But jobs like these, ones that presented a challenge while giving her creative freedom with her flowers and plants, were her favorite.

She tucked her phone into her pocket and stood, grabbing her wineglass.

"Have a good night."

"Are you staying here?"

A slight blush stained her cheeks as she followed his gaze to the empty glass in her hand.

"I'm not driving anywhere, if that's what you're asking. My place is just across the courtyard."

He looked at the double glass doors.

"Above the bookshop, I'm guessing."

"There's an apartment across the courtyard. Finn and Amanda live there, and I live in the studio above."

Another way her stepbrother and his fiancée had saved her. They could have easily rented the studio for a good price. Instead, they'd offered it to her for a song, enabling her to pour even more of her own money into The Flower Bell.

Grant stood, towering over her.

"I'll walk you to your door."

"It's literally across the courtyard."

"It's still New York City. The courtyard is dark, your stepbrother is busy and you've had at least two glasses of wine to drink." He crossed his arms. "It's non-negotiable."

She resisted rolling her eyes. Some things, at least,

didn't change. Even all those years ago, he'd been stead-
fast in walking her home, opening the door for her, little things that back then had made her feel cared for.

Now it grated on her. She'd been so willing to let everyone take care of her in the past. But she'd grown up a
lot. She'd lived in a couple of rundown apartments with
nothing but a dead bolt between her and some nasty
residents in the early years after her father's conviction.

Grant wouldn't care that she'd held her own against
mean drunks and lecherous louts. He'd argue with her
until she was blue in the face, and she didn't have the
energy for any more drama tonight.

"Fine. Thanks," she added grudgingly.

She dropped the glass off in the kitchen and waved
good-night to Amanda, who was still behind the register. Amanda glanced at Grant and then arched a brow.
Alexandra gave her a reassuring smile in return and a
thumbs-up as she and Grant stepped out into the quiet
darkness of the courtyard.

The glass doors closed behind them, shutting out
the music and conversation. Rain had turned to a light
mist as she crossed the courtyard, Grant two steps behind her. She tried to ignore the uptick in her heartbeat,
the quickening of her breathing, the awareness dancing
through her veins. It didn't help that, with the noise of
the bookshop gone and the only sound the distant hum
of New York traffic, the courtyard was suddenly a very
intimate space.

They were halfway across when thunder cracked
across the sky. A second later rain poured down in
sheets. Alexandra yelped in surprise as the icy-cold
downpour drenched her. Grant grabbed her hand and

dragged her across the cobblestones onto the tiny covered porch outside Finn and Amanda's apartment.

Alexandra stared out at the rain before glancing at Grant. She couldn't have held back her laughter if she'd tried. His perfectly styled hair was soaked, plastered to his forehead as he glowered at the rain.

"Something funny?"

His growl only made her laugh harder.

"I'm sorry," she gasped as she leaned against the brick wall. "It's just…you looked so perfect back there and now…"

"Now I look like a drowned cat?"

Just like that, her mirth disappeared as his lips curved into a ghost of the smile she'd fallen in love with all those years ago. It was a smile that had set her body on fire and made her heart soar.

He's your boss now, she sternly reminded herself. *Not your lover. Not anymore.*

"Something like that." She nodded to the pouring rain. "Finn has an umbrella inside his hall closet. I'll grab it for you."

"I don't need an umbrella."

"I didn't need to be walked across the courtyard, but here we are," she replied cheerfully as she pulled her key out of her back pocket. "Give me just a moment."

She hurried inside and pulled Finn's umbrella out of the hall closet. She started to smooth her wet hair off her face but stopped herself. What difference did it make what she looked like?

She stepped back out onto the porch. Heat scorched her cheeks as her eyes traveled from the state of his formerly styled hair to his body. His wet sweater had adhered to his chest, outlining every curve of muscle in lurid detail. Her lips parted as she remembered how he'd cradled her against his body after they'd first made love, her fingers curling in the dark hair on his chest as he'd traced his fingers across her shoulder, up and down her arm, over her belly. Each featherlight caress had simultaneously soothed the thundering of her heart while stoking the little flames left burning in the aftermath of their passion.

"Um, here."

She handed him the umbrella, keeping her eyes focused on the falling rain and off his perfectly toned abs.

Until his fingers brushed hers.

Sparks ignited and spread up her arm like wildfire. Her sharp intake of breath at the unexpected contact was surprisingly loud and echoed off the brick walls of the little porch. Her head jerked up. Grant's gaze was fixated on her, his body rigid. It was as if he'd turned to stone.

Whereas she felt horrifyingly, thrillingly alive for the first time in years. As if every nerve in her body had been brought back to life and was yet again responding to the man who had once brought her to heights of pleasure she hadn't imagined possible.

In the bookstore she'd mentally prepared herself before offering her hand in a gesture of professionalism. She'd also accepted her body's tingling response. Only natural when she was experiencing physical contact with her first, and only, lover after so many years. Her excitement over getting the contract, of finally having the possibility of saving her business, had been easy to focus on while dismissing the rest.

But now, with nothing between them but the coolness

of a rainy spring evening, she couldn't have stopped her body's response if she'd tried.

Grant yanked his hand back, the umbrella clenched so tightly in his grasp it was a wonder it didn't snap.

"Good night, Miss Waldsworth."

His frigid farewell immediately doused the fire ignited by that unexpected spark. She didn't respond as he opened the umbrella and walked across the courtyard without a backward glance. She waited until she saw him disappear within the bookstore before going inside.

The stairs up to her little studio seemed steeper that evening, creaking under the heavy weight of each step. The pale yellow walls of her apartment and the iron-framed bookcase overflowing with plants by the front door usually elicited a feeling of comfort when she'd return home. Tonight, however, they failed to induce even the smallest bit of joy as she walked in, tugged off her wet shirt and tossed it onto the tile by the washing machine.

She focused on the mundane tasks of getting ready for the night: watering her plants, washing her face, checking her email one last time for any orders.

It wasn't until she was curled up in her bed with a cup of steaming tea that she allowed herself to fully accept how much of a fool she'd made of herself. If there was anything more pathetic than showing a man how much she was affected by him, it was showing her former lover how much she was affected by him after he'd just literally rescued her business.

She hung her head. She'd pushed Grant out of her mind and out of her heart those first few years. Easy to do when just the thought of him had brought on a pain so sharp it made her feel like her heart was crack-

ing in two. With time, when little things like the scent
of roses or the music of a Ferris wheel reminded her of
happier days, she'd allowed herself a brief moment of
nostalgia before turning her attention to other things.

And when she'd seen Grant this morning, she hadn't
had time to examine how she felt about him. Every time
he'd crept back into her thoughts over the course of the
day, she'd banished him by focusing on her work.

Unfortunately, she now had all the time in the world
and a serious case of insomnia.

The dried violet petals she'd added to her tea drifted
in lazy circles in the cup. She didn't know how long she
stared at them, focusing on anything but the problem
she needed to confront, but by the time she finally took
a sip, the tea had turned cool and some of the petals had
sunk to the bottom.

Obviously, the physical attraction to Grant was still
there. *And why wouldn't it be?* she asked herself defensively. He'd matured into an even more handsome man.
They had a history. She'd attempted dating a few times,
but nothing had gone beyond kissing. It was only natural that her body would respond.

Slowly, cautiously, she examined her emotions, then
breathed a sigh of relief. She'd been mortified and re-
gretful, sad and resigned, even grateful, when Grant
had done the unthinkable and offered the contract. But
the rush of electricity and heat had been rooted in nothing but sexual attraction. There was no lingering hint
of love. How could there be when the Grant she'd seen
today was the complete opposite of the smiling young
man who had lit up every room he'd walked into?

Did I turn him into that?

She pushed that thought away as she turned off her

light and burrowed under the covers. The rain had abated but still fell steadily outside her window, a pleasant backdrop of noise as her eyes drifted shut.

Easier to focus on the shushing melody of rain and let herself drift into sleep than give voice to the lingering doubt that Grant had become so cold and reserved for one reason.

Her.

CHAPTER FIVE

GRANT PAUSED OUTSIDE the door of The Flower Bell. He'd been focused on his laptop and missed the details last night when his driver had taken him by, looking up only to see that her store was dark. The arrangements in the window were stunning, the logo crisp and neat. The door beckoned passersby to come in, a welcoming green with a white frame and a doorknob that looked as if it had been freshly polished.

A stark contrast to the rest of the shops lining the street. Most of the storefronts were empty with cracked windows and doors left ajar, as if their owners had fled so hastily one night they hadn't bothered to lock up. Hard to imagine that just a few blocks away the streets gave way to the more fashionable Greenwich Village district.

Rent in New York City was notoriously high. But was this truly the best Alexandra could do?

A siren screamed not too far away, followed by shouting. Grant frowned. He'd wanted to flaunt his success, yes. But this…this was far worse than he had imagined.

He opened the door and walked inside. The walls had been painted a misty gray that made the framed pictures of flowers on the walls jump out. A small chandelier hung over a round white end table flanked by two emerald wingback chairs. The album on the table was open to photos of various arrangements. Two refrigerators with glass doors took up most of the far wall, the bottom shelves filled with buckets of blooms and the top shelves with completed arrangements.

She'd done the best with what she had. But it would take more than a coat of paint and artsy photography to cover up the cracks in the walls, the signs of mildew in one corner and the harsh humming of the refrigerators.

Alexandra's back was to the door, her phone pressed to her ear as she scrolled through something on a laptop. She'd pulled her thick brown hair into a braid that nearly touched her waist and sported another T-shirt and jeans. A far cry from the brand-name clothes she used to wear. Yet, she wore it well, shoulders thrown back and her spine straight with a confidence she'd lacked when he'd first met her.

"I understand, but you're charging me almost what I'd pay in Greenwich."

Her voice whipped out, fierce and angry.

"I know most people wouldn't have given me the space, but—"

Her shoulders crept up toward her ears. Soft music drowned out most of the loud voice on the other end.

"But you told me the electricity would be fixed! I can't come in every morning wondering if my refrigerators are going to be out and all my flowers dead."

Curiosity morphed into quiet anger. He'd dealt with plenty of disreputable landlords in his time.

"I can't afford another thousand dollars!" A note of desperation crept into her voice. "Please, there must be something you can do. I have a big job that just came in, and I'm getting the first payment Friday."

The pleading in her tone catapulted him back into the past, to the night before Alexandra had turned on a dime and revealed her true colors. They'd been lying on the beach, sand and waves and her naked body bathed in silver moonlight, tangled up in each other after he'd made love to her on a silky blanket.

Let's run away.

He'd chuckled, one hand drifting lazily over her belly, the other cupping her breast. He'd asked where. She'd responded anywhere, as long as they could be together. At first, he'd thought she'd just been teasing. They hadn't discussed what would happen when the summer ended. But somehow, he would find a way to keep seeing her. He had another semester of school. He'd keep his search for graduate programs to New York City. He'd do anything to keep her in his life.

But she had turned to him, fingers fluttering against his face with an almost frantic energy as she'd suggested Paris, the Caribbean, South Africa, anywhere but the United States. Her questions had grown desperate, pleading, as she'd begged him to make a plan with her to escape so they could be together.

Except when he'd pressed her as to why, she'd shaken her head, bitten her lip and said she was being silly, that the thought of summer ending was making her melancholy.

And then she'd pushed him back onto the blanket, straddled him and eased herself down onto his hard length, chasing away his questions and destroying all rational thought.

The memory unsettled him. When she'd banished

him the next day in her father's library, he'd chalked up the incident on the beach as a spoiled heiress's melodramatic antics. That and his own unease that had lurked in the back of his mind ever since he'd met Alexandra, that he wasn't good enough for her.

Alexandra's voice broke through his thoughts.

"Look, I'm getting paid Friday. Either schedule the electrician to come in and start work or I walk." There was a burst of noise on the other end of the line, but Alexandra cut them off with an impatient jab of her hand. "I can walk because it's in my contract that you'll take care of associated utility repairs within fourteen days of my request. It's been eighteen days. This place sat empty for twelve months before I moved in. It's your choice if you want to lose a paying tenant."

Alexandra hung up the phone and swore under her breath. She turned around, her face paling when she saw Grant standing in the doorway.

"How long have you been standing there?"

"Long enough to know your landlord is a bastard."

His answer startled a small laugh from her.

"He is. A greedy one, too."

Grant cast an eye over the water stains on the ceiling and the peeling linoleum in the corner by the refrigerators. When his gaze landed back on Alexandra, she was watching him with pink cheeks, arms crossed defensively over her chest.

"I know. Location, location, location."

"Why here?"

The shrug she gave him failed to mask her embarrassment.

"Cheap. Available."

"You said most people wouldn't have given you the space."

The pink deepened into a fierce red as her eyes skittered away.

"You were standing there quite a while."

"Tell me what that meant."

Her head snapped back around, her eyes narrowing as she frowned at him.

"When did you get so bossy?"

"Answer the question, Alexandra."

She huffed.

"I tried renting a space near Finn and Amanda. The leasing agent was the daughter of one of my father's victims." Her voice dropped so low he could barely hear her. "Her father killed himself when he lost almost all of his retirement."

Damn it.

"That wasn't your fault."

The laugh that escaped her lips this time was bitter and thick with regret.

"Wasn't it, though, in some way? I knew firsthand what he was capable of. I overheard some of his business deals. I had my suspicions and I did nothing about it but wear my pretty clothes and take his money."

Self-loathing dripped from each word like poison. Grant stared at her, searching for any hint of deception. How many times had he challenged her on the way her father treated her? His employees? She'd acknowledged it but practically quaked at the possibility of confronting him.

Before he could question her further, she shook her head and frowned again.

"What are you doing here? I thought Jessica was supposed to take me out to the Hamptons house."

"She had other work today. I'm taking you."

Satisfaction threaded its way through his veins at the flicker of panic in Alexandra's eyes. After his nearly disastrous moment in the courtyard the other night, he'd needed to remind himself of why he'd booked her services in the first place. Which is why he'd opted to escort Alexandra out to the Hamptons house personally. It presented the perfect opportunity to not only give her a glimpse of the world he now lived in, but also a chance to remind her of her place in it.

"Oh."

"Is there a problem?"

"No, just…ah…no. Let me grab my bag and lock up."

As she turned off the lights, he cast one more critical glance over the shop. He'd wondered if his wealth would have any effect on the woman who had once spent her spring breaks in an overwater bungalow in the Maldives on a private island.

Judging by how far Alexandra had come down in the world, it wouldn't be hard at all to show her just what she'd given up.

CHAPTER SIX

ALEXANDRA STARED AT the house perched majestically above the deep blue waves of the Atlantic as the helicopter began its descent to the helipad in the corner of the estate. The architect had done an incredible job combining luxury with a homey feel. Pale gray shingles covered the exterior of the house. White shutters glinted in the sun. The darker gray roof topped three stories of what Grant had casually mentioned was a six-thousand-square-foot house, complete with twelve bedrooms, pool terrace, numerous decks and balconies in the same glimmering white as the shutters, and a private expanse of beach. All topped off by six acres of perfectly manicured grounds.

It came close to rivaling the Waldsworth Hamptons house, which had sat at the opposite end of the so-called Billionaires' Lane.

Just a few miles away. She kept her eyes trained on the grass rushing up to meet them and resisted the temptation to glance in the direction of her former house.

A house that, despite its grandeur and castle-like appearance, had felt like a prison until Grant had stumbled upon her in the gardens. That summer had been the happiest she'd ever been. She hadn't returned to the Hamptons since, the memories of what might have been too painful.

She should have made an excuse when she'd realized it was Grant and not Jessica she would be traveling with today. The tour would take less than an hour. It'd be enough time for him to show her where the various house party events would take place, and for her to take photos and notes and make sure the arrangement ideas she had would fit the space, lighting and atmosphere Grant wanted to create for his guests.

The sensation that someone was watching her penetrated through her melancholy. She looked up, but Grant's attention was focused on a tablet in his lap, a phone pressed to his ear. Almost the same position he'd been in since they'd walked out of her desolate little shop. The black limo that had awaited them at the curb had been modest in length but luxurious inside, a stark contrast to the worn-down appearance of The Flower Bell. She'd been well aware of the abrupt change in her surroundings, from the buttery leather seats to the granite and hardwood inlays that put the scarred countertops of the little kitchenette in her studio to shame.

Not to mention that she was in jeans, sandals and a blue T-shirt with The Flower Bell's logo on the front. Compared to Grant's three-piece dark teal suit and a gold tie that matched the Rolex on his wrist, she looked like…

Well, like Grant had when they'd first met. Although even in his white T-shirt and ripped blue jean shorts, he'd looked so handsome it had made her heart hurt. He hadn't leered or fawned or acted like a macho jerk. No, he'd just smiled down at her and stolen her heart on the spot.

She'd been so focused on how he'd made her feel, on how she felt about him, that she hadn't even wondered what he'd thought about the differences between them. Had he felt as uncomfortable as she did now when she'd taken him for a ride in her convertible along the shore? Or when she'd taken him to the beach party with her former boarding school friends who had name-dropped brands, exotic vacation locales and obscure food names in an attempt to shame "the gardener" she'd brought along?

Although, she remembered as she risked another subtle glance at Grant, he hadn't been fazed one bit. When she had paused, unsure how to handle their not so subtle snobbery without causing a scene, Grant had merely tightened his hold on her waist and calmly replied that he had preferred Cairo over Paris and that if they thought oysters Rockefeller to be a treat, they might want to broaden their horizons with Moqueca de Camarão stew with prawns. He'd said it all with a wide smile and steel in his eyes that had communicated he didn't give a damn how much money they had; he thought they were idiots.

And now, as he picked up the phone and rattled off a series of numbers to someone who sounded like a financial adviser, he had become one of them. Part of her was proud of him. He'd told her about growing up on the crowded streets of Fortaleza. His trips to exotic locations had been work trips with his father, overseeing the delivery of construction equipment to major worksites in Egypt, Morocco and Japan. Not the vacations her friends were used to going on, but Grant's father had made the most of the precious few hours of free time he'd gotten to share the world with his son.

"Hard work," he'd told her once. "But my father loved it. I think he took me along to show me what possibilities were out there, what I could do if I worked hard enough. And to make sure I didn't get pulled into the drug trade."

He'd spoken so matter-of-factly about it, told her the night of the bonfire about how he and his mother had fled Brazil after his father had resisted pressure from a local drug cartel to use construction equipment from the company he worked for to smuggle drugs into Europe, and paid for it with his life. His mother hadn't wasted any time in escaping to the US with her son before the cartel could come after them, too.

A fact her own father had held over her head days later when he'd told her that someone from the bonfire had told their parents, who had informed him that his daughter was "whoring herself to a common gardener."

"I'll be damned if the money I spent on your Ivy League education gets thrown down the drain so you can get pregnant by some opportunistic crook," David had said in that cold voice he used when he'd been trying to keep a hold on his temper.

"He loves me!" Alexandra had retorted in her first display of independence. "And I love him!"

Her father had laughed in her face.

"He doesn't love you, Alexandra. He loves your money and whatever you've been doing with him this summer that he could find with any other woman."

Still reeling from the harsh cruelty of his insults, she had scrambled backward when he'd stood and advanced on her, backing her into the shelves of the library.

"Break it off with him tomorrow or I will make sure

he and his mother are sent back to Brazil before the end of the weekend."

"He could be killed!"

Even now, the memory of her father's merciless smile made her shiver.

"That's the idea."

She and Finn had barely been talking at that point. She'd also realized, as she'd scrolled through her phone trying to think of someone who could help her, that she didn't have anyone other than Grant she could depend on.

A realization that had left her numb as she'd sat on her bed, surrounded by silk sheets, handcrafted Italian furniture and a balcony that overlooked the Atlantic. A princess trapped in a beautiful prison.

She'd stayed up late scouring websites, blogs, even contacted an immigration advocate organization the next morning. But she'd known the whole time that she was throwing pebbles against a giant stone wall. David Waldsworth had the money and contacts to make anything happen, including sending Grant and his mother back to face danger and possibly even their own deaths.

So she'd done it. She'd broken Grant's heart, and her own, to keep him safe.

Yet, she reflected as the helicopter touched down, had she really tried? She could make the argument that Grant's and his mother's lives had been at stake. But her whole life she'd been a doormat. Like at the bonfire, letting her former schoolmates say such hurtful things to the man she'd claimed to love. She hadn't been able to fully stand up to David until he'd been behind bars in an orange jumpsuit, cut off from the world and most of his resources that he could have used to retaliate.

She thought she'd grown stronger over the years. Standing up to her landlord and threatening to move out was not something the old her would have done.

But she'd still given in by moving in in the first place.

By the time the pilot circled around to open the door, she was thoroughly immersed in a pool of self-pity.

Great way to start off your first big job.

"Are you all right?"

She looked up to see Grant watching her with an eagle-eyed stare. She mustered a smile that probably looked as fake as it felt.

"Of course. Just thinking."

He knew she was lying. She could tell by the slight tightening of his lips, the deepening of the crinkles by his eyes. But he didn't pursue it. Instead, he hopped out and turned back, extending his hand to her.

She accepted his offer of help as she alighted from the helicopter…and nearly yanked her hand back at the sensual electricity that crackled between them. If she'd thought their accidental brushing the other night had been intense, it was nothing compared to the heat that swept through her body as his fingers closed over hers. Slowly, she looked up to see his gaze fixed on hers, fire burning so hot she could barely breathe. Was it anger making his eyes glimmer like molten amber? Or something else, something far more dangerous and intoxicating?

Somehow, she managed not to fall out of the helicopter, to place one foot in front of the other and step down to the helipad. Grant kept her hand in his until they reached the grass. He dropped her hand and turned to the pilot, conversing with him as if the world hadn't just trembled.

She turned away and faced the ocean. Maybe she should have gone on dates with some of the men Finn and Amanda had offered to set her up with. Maybe she should have tried to get out more. Because then she wouldn't be acting like she was still a nineteen-year-old college co-ed who couldn't get her first love out of her system.

Grant strode toward the house. She followed, widening her steps to keep up with his fast pace as they crossed the cobblestone driveway and walked up onto a stunning front porch, complete with thick pillars, white rocking chairs and fans that whirred lazily overhead.

"This is beautiful."

Grant looked over at her sharply before he nodded once. "Yes, it is."

He opened the door and gestured for her to step inside. Her mouth dropped open as she took in the soaring entryway, complete with dark hardwood and a white staircase that curled up to a loft lined with bookshelves. Unlike the home she'd spent countless summers in, this one combined elegance with a homey feel. The art on the walls blended shots of New York City and the Hamptons with pictures of Brazil.

Alexandra walked up to one photo of a footbridge painted a vivid red made all the more eye-catching by the brilliant blue sky behind it.

"That's the bridge at the Dragão do Mar, isn't it?"

Silence followed her question before Grant cautiously answered.

"Yes. My cousin sent me that photo."

Alexandra glanced over her shoulder, barely catching the flash of pain in his eyes before his billionaire's mask dropped back into place. An ache built in her chest. She had never had any emotional attachment to the places she'd lived. Even the Hamptons home, one that had been in the family for centuries, had been re-done so many times by David and the women parading through his life that all of its charm had been smothered by tasteless renovations.

What would it be like to have a home she missed so acutely? A loss made worse by the knowledge that she would most likely never be able to return without risking her life?

"It looks like an amazing place."

"It is." The ghost of a smile flickered about Grant's lips. "My father took me to the planetarium when it first opened. I'd never seen anything like it."

Before she could ask more, he stepped away and headed down the hall.

"We have thirty minutes before we have to fly back."

The moment of camaraderie evaporated as Grant walked briskly throughout the house. She focused on taking photos of the breakfast room, formal dining room, library, beach deck and the pool deck. She asked questions, took notes and showed Grant pictures of what she'd envisioned. His replies were direct and professional, with no hint of the fire she'd glimpsed out on the helipad. Whatever had been there had been brief. Perhaps he'd felt some of the sexual tension, or maybe he'd seen her wide-eyed reaction to his touch and been irritated by it.

They moved upstairs.

"There will be five couples, including one who is bringing their adult daughter, and another couple with teenagers. Laura Jones and several other executives will also be present off and on throughout the week. The four-person catering crew will be staying in the guesthouse."

Alexandra walked past the open doors of the guest rooms. It had been a long time since she had been surrounded by such luxury. Each one had been decorated individually, from pale blues to soft lavenders. All were welcoming and full of light from the numerous windows. Every suite had its own balcony and full bathroom, complete with marble jetted tubs. It would be easy to do arrangements for each room, with little tweaks for each morning so that guests would be greeted as they returned from breakfast with pleasant displays that matched the themes and colors of each room.

"The rooms are beautiful."

"They should be. Each cost a quarter of a million to renovate between the bathrooms, furnishings and balconies."

The facts were stated plainly. But even after all this time, she knew Grant and heard the faintest hint of smugness beneath the words. She glanced sharply at him. She'd been pleased when he'd offered her a tour of the house. It was much easier to design flowers for a space she'd experienced herself. Yet, ever since he'd had walked into The Story Keeper and offered to hire her, she'd wondered why. Why had he hired someone he obviously still loathed? Sure, she'd saved him a few thousand dollars, but he had millions at his fingertips.

As he pointed out several other customized features, including imported Italian marble in the shower, a nasty voice whispered that perhaps Grant had hired her for another reason entirely—to rub his success in her face.

No. Even though he wasn't bothering to hide his dislike of her, she couldn't imagine Grant hiring her just out of spite.

"You've accomplished a lot."

"I have."

"Is it enough?"

The question slipped out before she could stop it. *Too personal*, she thought frantically, but it was too late to take it back.

He blinked, then frowned. "Is what enough?"

She decided to go all in and gestured to the opulent wealth surrounding them. "All of this? The Pearson Group?"

"Of course. Aside from achieving my first billion, I've accomplished all of my goals."

She should be happy for him. But something in his words rang hollow.

"That's great."

His eyes narrowed. "What are you not saying?"

"It's none of my business."

"Spit it out, Alexandra."

His haughty tone made her throw caution to the wind.

"It just doesn't seem like you."

The thundercloud that gathered on his handsome face nearly made her take a step back. Foreboding washed over her.

"What doesn't seem like me?" His voice was deceptively soft, silky and menacing. "The success? The wealth? That people want to work with someone who started off as a mere gardener?"

Her heart clenched. The old Grant had been proud of his roots, uncaring about what others thought of him as long as he did his best. When had he started to care what others thought?

"No. I just remember you talking about starting scholarship programs for immigrant students, things like that."

"I've made millions in donations."

"And that's great." She put a hand to her forehead as a headache started to pound away at her temples. "You just seem more…removed. Like other things have become more important."

"I changed, Alexandra. You, more than anyone else, should know the reason why."

With that harsh parting shot ringing in the air, he turned and continued the tour. Alexandra stared at his back for a long moment. Her entire body ached for him, for everything he had given up on, the emptiness of his victories and, most of all, that he now saw his past and everything he'd overcome as weaknesses instead of incredible strengths.

"And your room will be around the corner in the other guest wing where the rest of the Pearson Group employees are staying."

She shook her head. She must have heard him wrong. "My room?"

He turned to face her, a slight wrinkle between his thick brows.

"Your room," he repeated slowly. "Is there a problem?"

"I just… I thought…"

That I wouldn't be staying under the same roof as you. That I would barely have to see you.

"Did you think you would commute from New York every day?"

"No. But I can get a room at a hotel—"

"All of my employees are staying at the house."

"Okay, but I'm not a regular employee."

Could he hear her panic? She didn't want to shell out the money for a hotel, but anything was preferable to being just steps away from where Grant slept, showered, dressed...

"This is non-negotiable."

The finality in his voice signaled she had two choices: accept the inevitable and suck it up for a week or kiss the contract goodbye. She blew out a harsh breath. Okay, so they would be staying in the same house. A house full of other people. And it wasn't like her room was next to his, or that he even liked her. No, his icy contempt was on full display.

"Fine." She managed to force a smile that probably looked more like a baring of her teeth. "Thank you."

Did she imagine the flash of triumph in his eyes? Whether she had or not, she certainly didn't imagine the nauseating feeling in the pit of her stomach. While this was different from her father, she didn't like submitting to someone else's power, feeling helpless and like her life was being arranged for her.

As she passed by the last room toward the back, she stopped, her queasiness disappearing as she stared in awe.

"Oh."

Whereas the other rooms would have fit perfectly under the definition of "relaxing" in the dictionary, this room combined quiet grandeur with a masculine touch. The walls were painted a light gray, except for the accent wall behind the bed that was comprised of dark wood. An industrialized black light fixture hung over the bed, which was a gargantuan piece of furniture covered in a slate-colored blanket. Six pillows, the cases smoothed to perfection, were lined up against the headboard.

But it was the pictures that caught her eyes, three above the headboard. She stepped into the room, her eyes soaking in the colorful photographs. In one, a man wearing an orange feathered headdress with a bright red band of paint covering his face stared into the camera, his eyes piercing through the picture. The one next to it featured a woman twirling in a blue dress with a giant silver bow on her chest, her smile still visible despite the white fringe that cascaded from her matching headdress over her face. The third portrayed a man in a green robe with a birdlike mask obscuring his face, a jeweled beak jutting out over his jaw and emerald feathers standing proudly up from the top of the mask as he held a matching scepter out to the photographer.

"Grant, these…these are incredible," she breathed.

The colors, the energy, all of it drew her in as she neared the photos, soaking in every detail. Her florist's mind matched the vivid hues to different flowers, creating arrangements in her head that would mirror what she saw.

"You won't need to do flowers for this room."

She turned, not bothering to hide her disappointment. "Why not?"

"It's my room."

The room shrank around them as she realized she was standing just a foot away from Grant's bed. She felt like an idiot. Of course it was his room. All of the other rooms were beautiful but lacked that personal touch of having someone who lived in them. Whereas this room… She glanced over her shoulder once more at the picture of the woman swirling in a circle, so carefree and happy in the midst of what looked like a very joyful celebration.

"I don't mind doing flowers for your room, too. In fact, I'd like to." She gestured at the photographs. "These would—"

"No."

Her head whipped around, blinking in shock at the amount of coldness in that one word.

"Why?"

"I'm your employer, not your friend. Not your lover," he added with punishing precision. "I don't need a reason."

No, he didn't, she acknowledged as she did her best to ignore the bite of his words. But something was going on. Could it be that he hadn't wanted her to see his private room? Or was it something to do with his home country, the pain she'd glimpsed in his eyes downstairs?

Once upon a time she would have gently pressed him, laid a comforting hand on his shoulder as he shared bits and pieces of himself. Once, he had told her the horrors of coming home to find his mother bent over his father's body, cradling him to her chest and sobbing like she would never know happiness again. Grant hadn't cried as he'd told the story in a monotone voice, but he had leaned into her embrace, buried his face in her hair and breathed in deeply. It had been the first time she'd felt strong for someone else, been their rock.

No more, she reminded herself as she glanced once again at the photos and then turned her back.

"No, Mr. Santos, you don't need a reason." She

looked down at her tablet, focused on the screen as she typed in a note. "No flowers for this room."

Silence settled, thick and heavy. She tucked her tablet into her bag and started for the door, keeping her gaze averted. She was embarrassed, yes, but also sad. The room reminded her of the man Grant had become: professional, cool and aloof. Yet, somewhere beneath that suave exterior she suspected still beat the heart of the man she had fallen for that summer; someone with a big grin who would have given anyone the shirt off his back.

She was so focused on her melancholy thoughts that she didn't notice Grant was still standing in the door, blocking her exit. She walked straight into his chest, stumbling backward when she hit six feet three inches of immovable billionaire. Grant grabbed her elbow to steady her, but the quick motion just made her tip forward as she tried to keep a hold on her bag.

She fell against him and his arm snaked around her waist. Awareness crashed over her like the waves smashing onto the beach, leaving her breathless as she stared at the tan skin visible at the base of his throat.

"I'm sorry," she squeaked. "I wasn't looking."

"I noticed."

She started to pull back, but his arm was like a band of iron. She swallowed hard and finally forced herself to look up. The gesture had the unfortunate result of bringing her mouth within a few inches of Grant's. Her eyes dropped down to his lips, firm and full. What would kissing him be like now? Would he still tease the seam of her mouth with his tongue, nibble on her lower lip until she gasped and granted him access, laughing as he kissed her senseless?

His head lowered, just a fraction, but enough to startle her and make her pull back. Her eyes jerked back up to his.

"You should be more careful, Miss Waldsworth."

This time she couldn't stop the hurt that swept through her at the use of her old name. If he hadn't made it abundantly clear that he thought of her as nothing but an employee, his continued use of her father's surname was the nail in the coffin. There would be no kisses, no moments of intimacy, no lovers' confessions. That was in the past.

Focus on your job.

"I will, Mr. Santos." She shook his hand off and stepped back, squaring her shoulders as she met his gaze head-on. "If you'll excuse me, I have more pictures to take."

He stared at her with that unflinching glower. But this time she didn't back down. He had put her in her place. She would stay there. But she would do a damned good job as the florist for the Pearson Group and show Grant and all of his wealthy guests what she was capable of.

At last, Grant stood to the side. She walked past him and continued down the hall without a backward glance. The flight back to New York would be awkward. But after that, she had no need to see him again until the brunch at the New York Public Library on Monday. After the brunch it would be the weeklong house party here, and then the gala at the Met the week after that. A busy schedule, but one that would keep her attention focused on her work and off the man she had once loved.

CHAPTER SEVEN

ALEXANDRA GLANCED DOWN at her watch as she walked
out of the Metropolitan Museum of Art. Her tour with
Jessica and Laura Jones had taken nearly two hours,
including an hour at the New York Public Library and
an hour at the Met, but it had been worth it. Unlike
with Grant's tour of the Hamptons house the day before, Alexandra had felt confident and in control. It had
only taken Laura two minutes to put Alexandra at ease,
and both women had responded to Alexandra's questions with detailed answers instead of Grant's short,
clipped replies.

She'd liked Laura almost immediately. But she
also liked Grant's executive assistant, she'd realized
somewhere between the Met's Great Hall, where the
guests would be welcomed, and the Cantor Roof Garden where, weather permitting, the cocktail hour would
be held. What she had initially perceived as Jessica's
cold exterior had masked a dry, witty humor and an
intelligent mind. Jessica's feedback on the prospective
clients in attendance and the whisperings she'd heard
about what people were already thinking of the Pearson Group had been invaluable.

Such as the concern that Grant hadn't come from

money. When Jessica had shared that bit, it had sparked a fierce defense inside Alexandra's chest. After everything he'd accomplished, after earning a graduate degree from Stanford and working for one of the most respected financial firms on the West Coast, people still looked down on him the same way her father had.

Her anger, fortunately, had also led to an idea for the breakfast at the New York Public Library that would kick off next week's schedule. The roses and hyssop were still a good fit for the centerpieces. But she wanted something even more impressive for the table where Jessica would be stationed at, something respectable and professional but also luxurious. Something people would take one look at and not only feel like Grant paid attention to the kind of details that would keep them swimming in their own money, but also that he could afford the kind of lifestyle he currently kept with or without them.

It probably wouldn't do much, she acknowledged. But doing something was better than doing nothing.

Being six o'clock on a Friday night, and with the first event taking place on Monday, that didn't leave her a lot of time to put something together. Hailing a cab proved difficult and by the time she reached her shop, it was after seven. She hurried inside and powered up her laptop. As it booted, she walked over to the small closet and opened it, eyes scouring the various vases she kept for displays and special occasions.

The bell dinged over the front door. Alexandra turned, her smile fading as she took in the stringy hair, torn clothing and shaky hands of the young man standing in the doorway.

"Are you okay?"

She froze midstep as the man reached into his jacket and pulled out a knife.

"Cash," he bit out in a grating voice.

"Sure. I have some in the register."

She raised her hands so that he could see she wasn't reaching for a phone or a weapon of her own. With slow, measured steps, she moved to the register, her eyes never wavering from the grimy knife clenched in his hand like a lifeline. She slid behind the counter, her fingers grasping for the key she foolishly kept in the lock of the register drawer. One twist and the drawer sprang open. She risked a glance down to scoop the meager pile of bills into her hands.

"Here."

She set the money on the counter. The thief darted forward, the knife still pointed in her direction, and used one hand to spread the bills across the counter. Her heart pounded, but she managed to keep her breathing even as his cracked lips moved, counting up the total.

He looked up, eyes narrowing in anger.

"More. I need more."

"That's all I have. Most people pay online."

"Then your laptop."

She paused. Logically, she knew she should hand it over. The computer wasn't worth her life. But in some ways, it was. The Flower Bell existed in that laptop, from her website and social media to client records and notes for all of her jobs. Because, like an idiot, no matter how many times Finn had reminded her, she hadn't backed up her files.

"Could I give you something else? There's some—"

"Laptop!" the man barked.

Before she could reply, he raised his hand over his head and then swung it down.

Grant instructed his limo driver to drop him off at the end of the block as he tucked the coat Alexandra had left at the Met over his arm. He wanted the element of surprise when he walked in the door. Petty, but he needed something to go his way. His ego still smarted over how yesterday had gone. Not only had showing off his wealth felt like a hollow victory, but they'd once again come so close to kissing and *she'd* been the one to pull away.

But yesterday, standing so close together in his bedroom, he'd been an inch away from scooping her into his arms and carrying her to bed. His body had throbbed with desire, a need to hold her in his arms once more and reacquaint himself with everything he'd missed the past nine years. The dip at the base of her spine that had always made her sigh when he'd kissed it. The smattering of freckles on her shoulders from all of the time she'd spent in the sun. The way she'd laughed when he'd kissed and nibbled his way up her legs, her chuckles turning to sighs as he'd trailed his lips higher toward the apex of her thighs.

Damn it.

What had seemed like her genuine reaction to the photos of Carnival had unsettled him. The couple of women he had brought to the Hamptons house since he'd purchased it had merely glanced at them before oohing and ahhing over the views, the pool, the caviar and the champagne enjoyed on the balcony. Symbols of who they thought he was, or at least the parts of him they were interested in: his money, his reputation, his connections.

That the first thing that had seemed to truly impress Alexandra had been his most prized possession in the house had unbalanced him. For those few minutes he'd been thrust back into the past, to a woman whom he felt had seen him, truly seen him, and loved all of him.

He inwardly swore. In the cold light of day, it had been easy to see that Alexandra had just been acting. He'd confided a lot to her years ago. It would make sense that, whether she was trying to save her business or worm her way back into his life, she would use what knowledge she had to wiggle past his defenses.

Next week was the biggest week of his life. And all he could think about was the past and what might have been. Which is why he was now spending his evening in a not great part of town so he could reestablish the boundaries that had nearly been undone instead of enjoying a glass of bourbon on the rooftop balcony of his penthouse. He determined the nature of their relationship, not she. Her reaction to the photos had thrown him off. He wouldn't be caught unawares again.

He'd arrived at the Met after she'd just left. His disappointment, he reassured himself, was because he'd wanted an opportunity to see her again in a professional setting, remind her that he was the one in control. When Jessica had handed him the threadbare raincoat Alexandra had left behind during her tour and told him Alexandra had mentioned running back to the shop to get some work done, he found the perfect excuse to see her before Monday.

His eyes moved back and forth over the darkening street as he neared The Flower Bell. Several streetlights were out, the bulbs most likely broken by vandals. The empty storefronts looked sad, paint worn by weather, time and neglect. It reminded him of some of the more downtrodden parts of Fortaleza.

Even though Fortaleza had its problems, the city had been good to him for most of his childhood. How many summers had he spent on the beaches to the south, hiking among the red cliffs that bordered the ocean with his father or snacking on *crème de papaya* under the palm trees with his mother? As his father's role in the construction company he'd worked for had grown, he'd taken Grant with him overseas when he oversaw the delivery of major orders. The locales had been incredible. But nothing had compared to coming home to Fortaleza.

Homesickness pricked him. It had been over twenty years since he and his mother had fled after their father had done the unthinkable and said no to a drug cartel that had wanted to use his construction equipment to smuggle cocaine to Belgium. The cartel had responded with a bullet and a notice that Grant and his mother would be next unless they helped. Jordana Santos had lived up to the meaning of her name—daring— and smuggled a twelve-year-old Grant out of the house under the cover of darkness. He had never learned how she'd done it, but less than a week later they'd arrived in New York City, where Jordana had channeled her grief at losing her husband into re-creating a life for her and her son. She lived a couple hours north of the city now, in a rambling Victorian with a garden out back where she drank tea, the occasional glass of wine and entertained her weekly book club.

A slow-paced, pleasant life. One she had more than earned. She turned down his offers of more—more trips, more clothes, more gadgets—with a soft smile. She told him the only thing that mattered to her was seeing him happy. A statement that, more and more, seemed to end on a question, as if she knew that his numerous successes hadn't yet delivered the happiness he sought.

But then she wasn't being completely honest with him, either. Yes, he knew he was the most important thing in her life. But returning to Brazil, seeing her family and friends, was a close second.

He would tell her in the fall that the head of the cartel that had ordered his father's execution had been killed, his organization taken over by a rival gang and moved to Natal. However, he wouldn't tell her the role he had played, that his interference time and time again in the cartel's operations had led to another organization moving in and taking care of someone they considered a weak link. He wanted to verify for himself that it was safe, take a trip before going with her again in the spring. He would not risk losing someone else. Losing his father, then Alexandra—or at least whom he thought Alexandra had been—had been painful enough. He would not risk heartbreak a third time by placing his mother in danger.

Oddly, the victory of his father's murderer being killed had felt unexpectedly hollow. Yes, one less drug dealer was on the streets. But it hadn't brought his father back. It had also left him restless, adrift, with nothing to focus his time, efforts, or money on. That restlessness had led to his next goals, of starting his own investment firm and achieving his first billion. Goals he was on the verge of realizing.

And Alexandra, damn her, had seen right through

him yesterday. His hands tightened around her coat. How had she known that the harder he pushed himself to succeed, the closer he got, the emptier he felt? As if he would always be pursuing something just out of reach?

Up ahead, a figure in a trench coat rushed out of The Flower Bell. The door slammed against the wall. Glass shattered and rained down on the pavement. The figure glanced back into the shop before running down the street, arms pumping, something flat and metallic clutched in one hand.

His body roared to life. He stepped in front of the person and dropped into a crouch, his years of high school wrestling coming back as he surged forward, grabbed the runner around the waist and stopped him cold. Whatever the man had clutched in his hands dropped to the pavement as Grant swung him around and pinned him against the wall.

"Let go of me, man!"

Sweat and an all too familiar bleach-like scent stung his nostrils. Older boys in his neighborhood in Fortaleza had started to carry that smell on them when they started working for the cartels.

"What were you doing in The Flower Bell?"

The man finally lifted his head. Bloodshot eyes sat deep in a face with skin stretched so tight Grant could see the outline of his bones. The man smiled, revealing chipped, yellowed teeth.

"Just getting some flowers."

Grant glanced down, his blood turning cold as he realized what lay on the ground between them.

"Where did you get that laptop?"

The man wasn't high enough to miss the danger in

Grant's voice. He shrank back against the wall."Look, man, I don't want any trouble—"

A high-pitched siren cut off whatever the junkie had been about to say. Grant's head whipped around, his heart tripling in speed as a police car stopped in front of The Flower Bell and two officers got out.

"Officer!" he shouted.

They glanced at him, then did a double take as they took in the scene. Another siren sounded in the distance.

"Go help him," the female officer ordered her partner before she entered The Flower Bell.

It took every ounce of self-control Grant possessed not to toss the struggling addict at the officer approaching and rush inside. Once the officer handcuffed the thief, Grant scooped the laptop off the pavement with one hand and ran to the store just as an ambulance pulled around the corner.

No.

Past met present as the sirens and flashing lights sparked a cascade of memories: walking up to his house, seeing his mother cradling his father's body in her arms, the shriek of the sirens as the ambulance had arrived far too late to do anything but take him away covered by a sheet.

Por favor, não.

He burst into the shop, his chest so tight he could barely breathe.

Alexandra sat on a stool next to the counter, wincing as the officer placed a cool rag against a red gash on her forehead. Fury pounded in his ears with a roar that blocked out all sound.

She could have been killed.

Dimly, he heard his name.

"Grant?" She blinked, shook her head and then winced. "Sorry. Mr. Santos. What are you doing here?"

"You were just attacked and robbed, Alexandra. Screw the Mr. Santos."

The roll of her eyes reduced some of the tension in his shoulders.

"Okay, Grant, what are you doing here?"

"You forgot your coat at the Met."

She frowned and looked down. When she saw the laptop in his hands, her eyes brightened.

"You got my computer back!"

She started to get up, but the officer laid a hand on her arm.

"Ma'am, you need to get checked out by the paramedics first."

"I'm fine," she protested. "He whacked me on the head, but it's okay."

"It's not okay."

Both the officer and Alexandra looked up as Grant's words whipped out with ferocious intensity.

"It's not okay that he hit me, no, but my head just hurts a little. I'll be fine—"

"You're going to the hospital," Grant cut in.

The officer frowned. "Ma'am, while I think someone could use a lesson on manners, I agree with him. A head injury is nothing to mess with. Once the shock wears off, the pain might be more than you expect."

Alexandra's eyes found Grant's again and she sighed. "Fine."

It was after midnight when Grant's limo pulled up outside the bookstore. He took one look at Alexandra curled up in her seat, eyes barely open and skin so pale it looked like snow, and made a split-second decision.

"Ralph, go home. I'm going to take Miss Moss up to her apartment and stay with her tonight."

Ralph didn't even blink an eye.

"Yes, sir."

"You are not staying the night," Alexandra protested feebly as she moved to unbuckle her seat belt. "I'm fine."

"You look like hell," Grant replied bluntly before he got out and circled around the limo. He opened the door, reached in and hauled Alexandra into his arms. She gasped as she grabbed on to the lapels of his coat.

"What are you doing?"

"Carrying you."

"I can walk, you know. I got hit in the head, not the legs."

"You're also on strong painkillers after going through a hellish experience. Your stepbrother and his fiancée are out of town, and you told me yourself there's no one else to call." A point that had relieved him when the doctor had asked if there was anyone she could contact. Not that Alexandra's romantic life was any of his concern. They weren't together. But the thought of her being with anyone had sent jealousy slithering through his veins.

"Either I carry you up to your apartment or you're fired."

She huffed but didn't call his bluff. As he walked through the little alley next to the bookstore that led to the courtyard, her head drooped onto his shoulder. The heaviness of her head against the crook of his neck made his arms tighten around her as the reality of what he was doing fully sank in.

He was holding Alexandra in his arms once more. Her head lay where it so often had after they'd made love, as her fingers had traced soft patterns on his chest or she'd stretched up to plant a gentle kiss on his jaw. He'd had lovers before her, and two lovers in the years after he'd left New York. Pleasurable experiences, but none had come even close to the kind of emotional intimacy he and Alexandra had shared. That he had been her first, too, had brought out a fiercely protective side of him that hadn't existed with any of his other paramours.

A protective side she had adored. But tonight, until now at least, she hadn't seemed to need him. She'd stood up to her attacker, dialed 911 and, instead of breaking down in tears and turning to him for comfort like she would have in the past, she'd stayed strong and independent.

Her show of strength had ensnared him. Alexandra had been beautiful and sweet and kind that summer so long ago. But she'd also struggled with standing up for herself, preferring to withdraw or smile and nod instead of creating a scene. He couldn't picture Alexandra Waldsworth keeping calm during an attempted robbery, nor handling the aftermath with such aplomb.

But Alexandra Moss had done just that. She'd answered the doctor's questions, submitted to the CT and MRI scans Grant had insisted on to verify that she didn't have a concussion and argued with him when he'd provided his billing information.

"That's ridiculous!" she'd snapped as the charge

nurse's head had swung back and forth between them like she was watching a tennis match. "I can pay for myself."

"Except you can't," Grant had fired back. "And you went back to the shop to do something for the job I hired you to do, making you my responsibility."

"I can take care of myself, *Grant*."

He'd gotten his way. But it had taken much more of a fight than he'd expected.

At first, it had been a relief to see that, aside from the nasty bruise developing on her forehead, she was okay. Then it had irritated him. He hadn't been terrified in a long time. Not since that first year he and his mother had barely scraped by in a crappy apartment on the Lower West Side and every knock on the door had made him reach for a baseball bat, convinced the cartels had arrived to finish what they'd started.

But it hadn't just been the initial fear when he'd realized something bad had happened inside The Flower Bell that still troubled him. Now it was the fear that he was worrying about Alexandra, admiring her strength, caring about her recovery. No matter what way he examined the issue, his feelings were undeniable.

Undeniable, but certainly not part of his plan.

Alexandra's head drooped, then snapped back up as they entered the courtyard. There would be time for him to dissect this new development later. Now his first priority was getting Alexandra up to her bed so she could rest and heal.

"My key…"

"Where is it?"

She fumbled in her pocket and produced a silver key on a chain. He leaned down enough for her to insert the key in the lock and turn the knob, then kicked the door shut behind them and started up the stairs.

"You can put me down now."

Judging by the slur in her words, the pain medication mixed with the sleeping pill the doctor had prescribed was having the desired effect.

"You'd probably fall down the stairs."

"Would not," she mumbled back as she burrowed closer to him, her face nuzzling his chest.

Querido Deus. He hardened at her touch, his arms tightening around her slender body as they neared the landing. He belonged in hell for even contemplating anything remotely sensual after the evening she'd experienced. But he couldn't stop the rush of possessiveness that flooded his body with an old yet all too familiar heat.

The door to her apartment was unlocked. A good thing, too, because judging by the heaviness of her breathing and the limpness of her body, she had fallen asleep. He walked inside, noting details like the frayed furniture and worn rug along with the unexpected homey touches. The Alexandra he'd pictured these past few years—the too many times he'd thought of her— would have found some way to live in luxury, whether that was living off whatever the government had left her after exhausting her family's finances to pay back her father's victims, or finding herself a new beau with the income to keep her in her preferred lifestyle. He'd never imagined an apartment like this, much less the care that had gone into making it a home, evident from the plants lined up on the windowsill to the cozy egg chair arranged next to a shelf crowded with what looked like used books. Not the untouched rare editions that had crowded the mahogany shelves of David Waldsworth's library in the Hamptons where Alexandra had broken up with him, but books with cracked spines and worn pages. Books that had been read and loved.

He walked over to the bed, his head spinning with a question that had been haunting him ever since Alexandra had walked back into his life last week: Who was she? Every time he thought he had an impression of who she had been and who she'd become, she turned around and surprised him.

He eased her down onto the lavender sheets with infinite care. The bed sagged slightly beneath her weight, a sign of its age. He frowned as she shivered and glanced at the thermostat. It was set fairly low for a chilly New York spring. He grabbed a blanket off the egg chair and covered her. There had been plenty of winters when his mother had kept the heat low, or opened windows in the sweltering heat of summer instead of turning on the air-conditioning, to save money. As soon as he'd banked his first major profit from his investments, he'd bought her the Victorian house in New York's wine country equipped with the luxuries people dreamed of, like a private pool, and the luxuries they took for granted, like a working furnace and a refrigerator that never gave out.

Yes, he knew the realities of living without all too well. But seeing Alexandra skimping on basic necessities like a comfy bed and heat bothered him. Just like her shop. She'd obviously done what she could to make it look as presentable and professional as possible. Unfortunately, it would take more than her meager attempts at decorating to erase the reality of its location,

or for her to continue to draw in business from the kind
of clients she was trying to attract.

Not your problem.

He had to keep perspective. Just because they'd
shared something once, just because Alexandra might
have changed and grown during their time apart, meant
nothing. He had a company to launch and a fortune to
make. Alexandra had a business of her own to save.
Even if she had changed, even if he could begin to understand why she'd done what she had all those years
ago, how could he ever let himself trust her again?

He started to stand up as Alexandra rolled over and
let out a soft sigh.

"Grant."

Temptation reared and threatened to pull him under
as the devil on his shoulder coyly whispered in his ear,
encouraging him to lie down next to her for just a moment.

He stood up and stalked across the room, throwing
himself into the chair by the bookshelf. He would stay
until dawn in case she needed him during the night.

It was a hell of his own making, he realized ten minutes later as she sighed in her sleep and rolled over
again, leaving a tempting empty space next to her. He
had been the one to insist on accompanying her home,
to carry her upstairs, to put himself in the role of hero
when it was becoming clear that the last thing Alexandra needed was someone to take care of her. She had
grown into an independent, determined young woman.

Or, he wondered as he dropped his head back against
the chair frame, had she always been this way? She'd
certainly appeared strong the night she'd broken his
heart. Had this thread of steel always existed beneath

her beauty and he'd just been so intoxicated with their summer romance that he'd missed who she really was?

The never-ending question rotated around and around in his mind as sleep finally overtook him. His last image was of Alexandra curled up in her bed, her face peaceful and a small smile playing about her lips.

CHAPTER EIGHT

ALEXANDRA PLACED THE last bouquet in the refrigerator and surveyed the white cymbidium orchids framed by red roses with a critical eye. Tomorrow Grant's exclusive guests would arrive between noon and five to fresh flowers in their rooms, followed by a cocktail reception and a dinner on the patio. It would be a nonstop whirlwind, but a welcome one. The hectic schedule meant less time to think about everything that had transpired the past few days.

Saturday morning she'd woken to a splitting headache, pain pills on her nightstand and a glass of water. Grant had left no sign that he'd even been in her apartment, save for the lingering scents of cedar and amber that clung to her body no matter how hard she'd scrubbed in the shower. She'd been torn between embarrassment that she'd been so far gone after her trip to the hospital that she'd allowed him to care for her like that, and savoring the brief flashes of memory she had of him carrying her in his arms and laying her on the bed.

She'd somehow hauled herself to the shop Saturday afternoon. She'd managed the few orders that had trickled in for dates, graduations and nearly forgotten anniversaries as she had worked on the arrangements for the Monday morning brunch. Sunday had been busy, too, with finalizing everything for the week ahead and posting two part-time positions made possible by her initial payment from the Pearson Group. She would have loved to have Sylvia back, but her former employee had already found a new role. The wholesaler who provided her biweekly flower order for the shop had set her up with a floral company in East Hampton that would make daily deliveries to Grant's mansion for her week away. It was a lot of details flying around at once, more than she'd ever had to coordinate in her six months of operating The Flower Bell.

But it had been worth it. She'd arrived at sunrise to the library, a staff member's grumpy face softening into a smile when she'd handed her a small bouquet of daisies. She'd learned over the years that having extra arrangements, even something as simple as daisies, could make all the difference when working with the often overlooked employees who made magic happen behind the scenes of events like weddings and graduations. The employee had clutched the daisies in her hand as she'd escorted Alexandra to Astor Hall, a white marble hall with soaring archways and a grand staircase that swept up to the second floor. The tables and chairs had already been arranged, leaving it to Alexandra to adorn the tables with the hyssop and rose design she'd first showed Grant in his office two weeks ago.

As she'd left, she'd deposited one last arrangement on the welcome table at the base of the stairs: burgundy roses, violet-hued dahlias, seeded eucalyptus and purple cymbidium in a silver vase she'd picked up at an estate sale last summer. Lush, vibrant but still elegant. It also drew the eye to the table Jessica had set out with materials on the Pearson Group's offerings, as well as framed biographies of Grant and the other executives he'd brought on board.

Alexandra had glanced around the hall to make sure she was alone before she'd peeked at Grant's biography. Jessica had asked her opinion on Friday about three different photos. Two had been professional headshots, both featuring an unsmiling Grant. In one he'd looked directly at the camera, eyes slightly narrowed, lips set in a firm line. The other had him looking at something off camera. It had illustrated his incredibly handsome profile. But both had looked posed and insincere.

The last one, the one Alexandra had recommended and Jessica had gone with, had been of Grant caught in midlaugh, his eyes crinkled as he'd chatted with a group of investors at some event at his old job in California. He'd been surrounded by people of all different ages and backgrounds who were also smiling, their attention fixed on him. She'd traced a finger over his smile. It had been so long since she'd seen him smile like that.

She'd walked out of the library just as the caterers were arriving to set up and immediately departed for the Hamptons, grudgingly accepting the helicopter ride Grant had offered so she skipped traffic and had as much time as possible to work on her flowers. The afternoon had then been spent putting together the guest room arrangements and the Juliet garden roses that would be featured throughout the house. The sun had been setting as she'd finished placing red and pink zinnias into round glass bowls with tangles of ivy cascading from the rims that would take center stage during dinner on the deck that overlooked the pool and the endless expanse of ocean just beyond.

She was exhausted. And proud. This was what she had envisioned when she'd opened The Flower Bell. Long days and sometimes even longer nights full of blooms, greenery and endless opportunities to take an event from nice to extraordinary.

With a smile on her face, she closed the door to one of the four floral refrigerators Laura Jones had rented to house the flowers in the finished basement. She walked up the stairs, past the walk-in pantry that was the size of her suite upstairs and into the massive kitchen. Beyond the picture-perfect deck, infinity pool and white picket fence, the waves of the Atlantic rolled up onto the private beach.

Perhaps she would make herself a sandwich and eat it out on the deck, soak up the brief moment of aloneness before the chaos of tomorrow…

She uttered a shriek as a shadow detached itself from the wall.

"Grant!" *Damn it*. She mentally kicked herself. "Mr. Santos. You startled me."

"My apologies."

The hint of a grin lurking about his lips punched through her defenses.

Be professional. Don't give in.

"No apology needed. It's your house. I just didn't expect you until tomorrow."

Grant advanced into the kitchen, his broad frame and commanding presence filling the space.

"I wanted to be on site in case anything required my attention before the guests arrive."

"Ah."

"Still working?"

"Just finished. I'll have all the guest room flowers

out by eleven, and the cocktail tables ready by five."
She pulled out her phone and started to pull up the
schedule. "I'd prefer to wait until as close to seven as
possible to put out the dinner flowers. It's going to be
warm tomorrow and—"

"I trust you, Alexandra."

Her fingers tightened around her phone. She had
never expected to hear those words from his lips again.
Apparently, he hadn't, either, because he looked mildly
surprised at contradicting himself so quickly after telling her he wanted her to report directly to him so he
could keep her in line.

Although, she realized, he had seemed...softer toward her since the attempted theft at The Flower Bell.
Part of her wanted to think that maybe they were finally
moving beyond the hurdles of the past. Or perhaps he
just felt sorry for her. Whatever the reason, having him
look at her with something akin to friendliness instead
of cold derision had been a welcome change.

"Well...thank you."

"Have you eaten?"

The words had barely been spoken when her stomach let out a loud growl. Heat bloomed in her cheeks
as he chuckled.

"I'll take that as a no. I didn't have time to grab dinner before I left New York City. Sara usually leaves a
plate of cold cuts and fruit in the fridge if she knows
I'm coming."

Alexandra had met Sara, the housekeeper, earlier. A
smiling woman with a booming voice that belied her
petite stature and a long brown braid that stretched past
her waist, she'd oohed and aahed over the flowers to the
point that Alexandra hadn't been able to resist sending

her home with one of the spare bouquets she'd brought for the cocktail hour. Sara's effusive praise had been worth the little niggle of worry that something would go wrong tomorrow, and she'd regret giving away the spare.

But, she reminded herself, that was part of the business, part of what she'd worked so hard on over the past few years. Before, when things went wrong, she'd always had someone around to fix things for her to the point she'd been nearly helpless. As she'd slipped from the world of wealth and glamour to a simpler existence, she'd been confronted with how much she had taken for granted. Big things like managing a budget or little things like making her bed or scrubbing the floor in her kitchen. The first time she'd deep cleaned her studio and stepped back to survey her work, she'd felt prouder of the scarred yet shiny wood floors than she had ever felt of the trophies and medals strategically placed in her father's library from the numerous activities he'd enrolled her in.

Giving something as simple as a bouquet of flowers to someone as kind and jovial as Sara was worth a little bit of stress if it kept her tethered to the real world and reminded her of who, and what, was important.

"I met Sara earlier. She's very kind."

A frown crossed Grant's face.

"Yes, she is."

Alexandra smiled.

"You say that like it's a bad thing."

"Not a bad thing, just…" Grant rubbed the back of his neck in a gesture that almost seemed self-conscious. "I always thought of her as efficient. But she is kind."

"Efficient is a good trait, too."

"It is." He moved to the refrigerator in the kitchen, one of two set into the wall. "Would you like a glass of wine, too?"

It suddenly dawned on her what Grant was offering.

"You...you want to eat together?"

He glanced over his shoulder, one eyebrow arched.

"Was that not clear?"

"I don't think employers and employees usually eat together, so no. I thought you were just offering for me to dig around in your fridge."

Grant grimaced as he reached in and pulled out the plate he'd mentioned. More like a platter, a silver one with curved handles and covered in berries, slices of cheese and meat, olives, artisanal crackers and several little bowls of various dips.

"I was overly harsh during our tour. My bedroom is a private space, one I hadn't intended on sharing."

His explanation both mollified and saddened her. Not only was it a private space, but he also probably didn't appreciate having an ex-lover who had ended things in such a spectacularly horrible fashion invading his sanctuary.

Yet, at one time she would have been one of the few people invited into that space. Just another reminder that staying the course and keeping things professional over the next two weeks was in both their best interests.

He set the platter on the table and pulled out two plates and a bottle of wine.

"Sara always makes enough to feed at least three people. But it gives me something to pick at for a day or two."

He poured the wine, golden liquid bubbling inside the glasses.

"Champagne?" Alexandra asked as she lifted the glass to her lips, the bubbles tickling them.

"It's a sparkling chardonnay from Rio Grande do Sol. Brazil has set itself apart as one of the top exporters of sparkling wine in recent years."

Alexandra grinned at the pride in his voice. She took a sip, her eyes widening as a light sweetness hit her tongue.

"It's delicious."

Grant's smile hit her hard. Genuine, broad and full of happiness. It transformed his face from broodingly attractive and mysterious to devastatingly handsome. It was also, she realized, the first time he had looked truly happy since they'd become reacquainted.

"My cousin's winery. She's well on her way to becoming a success."

A question jumped into her head, nearly spilling from her lips before she bit it back. She glanced down at the plate Grant had pushed toward her and popped a juicy grape into her mouth instead.

"What?"

She looked up to find him staring at her. She swallowed the grape too fast and descended into a coughing fit. Grant circled the kitchen counter and pressed her wineglass into her hand. The wine soothed her throat while giving her a pleasant burst of light-headedness that eased some of the tension in her chest.

"Nothing."

"We may not have seen each other for a long time, Alexandra, but I know when something's on your mind."

She thought about denying it, but what would be the point? One, she'd be lying, and she'd done enough lying to Grant to last a lifetime. Two, he did know her, better than anyone else.

"The photos in your room…they're from Brazil."

He nodded once. "From Carnival. An annual celebration, similar to your Mardi Gras."

"Do you miss it? Your country?"

He exhaled sharply, staring down into his wineglass before nodding again.

"Every day." He walked over to the window and looked out at the dark sea. "I've spent more of my life here in the United States than in Brazil, but it's like a piece of me is missing. My mother and father's families, my heritage…all of it is back in Fortaleza."

Had she thought her heart broken before? Because her personal pain, caused by her own inability to stand up to her father, was nothing compared to the horrors Grant had experienced at such a young age. Horrors that continued to haunt him.

"Do you think you'll ever go back?"

He swirled the wine in his glass, held it up to the window and watched as the golden liquid circled about.

"I plan on returning later this year, after the Pearson Group launches. If the trip goes well, my mother and I will go back together next spring."

Her mouth dropped open. Fear rushed through her, momentarily robbing her of her voice.

"What?" she finally gasped. "But…you told me you and your mother could be killed."

He turned back to her, a vengeful gleam of satisfaction glinting in his tawny gaze.

"The cartel that executed my father was brutal but small, disorganized. Once I started building up my personal wealth, it wasn't hard to interfere. A delayed shipment here, police interfering there. Word got around that the man who killed my father wasn't reliable, that he might have even been working with the police. He was killed last year, and the cartel disbanded."

A shiver crept down Alexandra's spine as another question whispered through her mind.

"I didn't have him killed," he said softly, answering her unasked question.

She blinked, her lips parting.

"I… Grant, I don't—"

"You wondered. I did, too, as I accrued my wealth. Would I kill him if I got the chance?" He took a deep, long drink of his wine. "I always told myself I wanted to be rich so I could ensure my mother and I never had to go without again. We weren't wealthy in Brazil, but life was pleasant. Here, in the States, with nothing but grief and a cramped apartment…" His voice trailed off as he revisited the past in his head. "But it wasn't just for my mother. I knew if I made enough, became so rich no one could touch me, I could wipe out the cartel that killed my father."

She stared at him, confused. Bitterness coated his tone. How was taking out an organization that had caused so much pain and suffering a bad thing? He'd been a child on the verge of manhood who'd had his youth ripped from him, been torn from his home and the rest of his family that could have supported him and eased his transition into life without his father. Who wouldn't envision revenge?

"Now that you know, you probably see me as belonging in this world even less."

"What?"

Grant chuckled, the sound harsh and hollow.

"Don't deny it. I made the cartel weak. I created the situation that gave another group the nerve to kill the man who ordered my father's death. And I was glad when he died. I might wear the right clothes, drive the right cars, but underneath it all, you still see me as nothing more than common street trash."

"Don't put words in my mouth," she retorted. She set her wineglass down harder than she'd intended, the clink of glass on marble echoing in the kitchen. "Do you want to know what I'm thinking? The last time I saw my father in prison, he was vicious and nasty and cruel. I visited him every week for months like a good daughter, and the bastard never let up on all the ways I'd failed him." She circled the island, anger charging through her veins. "I walked away to him shouting at me to come back, to stop being a doormat, and all I could think was how I hoped he would die in prison." She stopped a few feet away from him, furious at the cartels that had stolen so much from Grant, at her father, at Grant himself for thinking the worst of her and, of course, at herself. Always that self-loathing lurking in the background of everything she did.

"So no, I don't think you're a monster, Grant, for wanting to avenge your father's death and make it safe for you and your mother to return to your country while stopping a drug cartel from hurting more people. Or for being happy that your father's killer is dead. I think you're a perfectly normal, rational human being who actually did something with his life, and it's about damn time you gave yourself some credit for everything you've achieved instead of doing what I imagine you've been doing for the last nine years and wondering if you're just as bad as the cartel, because you're not."

Grant set his wineglass down on the island and turned to her, his gaze impenetrable.

"Is that how you really feel, Miss Moss?"

It took a moment for his use of her preferred name to register. When it did, it cooled some of her anger and thrust her into a state of confusion.

"Yes."

He closed the distance between them until only a sliver of light separated their bodies. The heat of her anger morphed into sensual awareness that tightened her muscles into tense coils. She hated how quickly her breathing roughened, how easily he could probably perceive the effect he had on her. But there was no stopping it. He had always made her feel like this, ever since he'd smiled down at her in the gardens and made her heartbeat quicken into a thundering gallop.

"Good to know."

His lips closed over hers with a searing possessiveness that made her gasp. As soon as her lips parted, his tongue darted inside her mouth and laid claim to her body once more. She didn't waste any time in wondering whether this was a good idea or not, in questioning what was happening. Not when all she wanted was to feel him, just once more.

She flung her arms around his neck and returned the kiss with all the pent-up desire and emotion she'd suppressed the past nine years. Grant groaned her name. His hands closed around her waist, and he lifted her onto the counter. He nudged her legs apart and stepped between them. She moaned as his hips pressed into hers, the hardness of his erection setting her body on fire as she squirmed against him.

"Grant," she whispered into his mouth. "Grant, please…"

Her hands moved up to his face, her fingers settling on the curve of his jaw, the sharp cut of his cheekbones, reacquainting herself with the familiar and exploring everything she had missed as he plundered her mouth with devastating skill.

One of his hands moved to her back, his fingertips searing her skin through the thin material of her shirt. The other cupped her face as he urged her closer. Tears pricked her eyes. Even with the frantic passion building between them, the old intimacy that had drawn her to Grant, that union of souls and knowing that no one else could possibly know her and love her as he had, still burned as brightly as it had all those years ago.

Dimly, she heard a door close, followed by someone calling out Grant's name. She yanked back at the same time Grant did. They both stared at each other, chests heaving, eyes wild as they stared at each other with a mixture of lust and shock.

"Mr. Santos?"

Jessica.

Alexandra scooted off the counter, moved around Grant and ducked into the pantry seconds before she heard the telltale click of high heels on hardwood as Jessica entered the kitchen.

"Good evening."

Grant's greeting went unanswered for a moment. Alexandra scooted deeper into the pantry, her heart pounding. So much for acting like a professional. She'd just made out with her boss on his kitchen counter the night before a week that could make or break her business. And now she was hiding.

Running away, like you always do. You haven't changed.

"Good evening." A faint rustling reached Alexandra's ears. "The items you requested. I'll do an inventory before bed and meet with Miss Jones, Miss Moss and the catering team first thing in the morning."

"Thank you, Jessica."

Another pause. Alexandra glanced over her shoulder, her eyes alighting on the doorway that led to the back staircase. She moved toward the door with cautious steps.

"You're welcome, sir. Have a good night."

Was that smugness in Jessica's tone? Surely not. As much as Alexandra had enjoyed her tour with Jessica at the library and the Met on Friday, the woman didn't seem capable of deviating from her clipped monotone.

Jessica's clicking heels faded as she moved out of the kitchen. Alexandra hustled to the door and hurried up the back stairs. She didn't want to know if Grant came after her or not. His unburdening of himself in the kitchen, her unprofessional confrontation and their searingly hot make out session on the kitchen island had not been part of her evening plans.

She made it to her room and closed the door, sagging against it as she closed her eyes. It was completely foolish to give in so quickly to the desire Grant had inspired in her. Even more foolish to show him once again how much he still affected her. He trusted her to provide flowers for his events, but like he'd said at the bookstore, he didn't trust *her*, would never be able to trust her. She still doubted and questioned her motives, her abilities, her decisions. How could she possibly ask him to do more than she could do for herself?

And she would never be able to fully forgive herself

for the past. Aside from the lust straining both their fortitudes, there was nothing between them except a painful history that could never be repaired.

Tomorrow. Tomorrow was an opportunity to start fresh. Tomorrow she would keep her distance, behave professionally and, above all, avoid late-night kitchen assignations with Grant Santos.

CHAPTER NINE

THE SETTING SUN lit up the sky with a dazzling display of rosy pink, vibrant orange and soft violet. Upbeat jazz pulsed through speakers strategically placed around the deck. Guests mingled among the three round tables that had been set up with the zinnia arrangements proudly on display among the white and blue china plates, elegant glassware and flickering candles.

Alexandra stood off to the side, conscious of the curious glances occasionally tossed her way. She didn't recognize anyone from her days in the Hamptons, thankfully. But she still felt unsure of herself.

And uncertain why she was here.

It had been Jessica who had insisted she stay for the dinner. It had come up that morning when they'd been doing the final walkthrough of the schedule. Mercifully, if Jessica had suspected anything last night, she'd kept it to herself.

"After dinner you'll be on the deck to welcome guests with Ms. Jones and the other Pearson Group executives—"

"Oh, no," Alexandra had cut in. "I'll just go up to my room or wander the grounds. I don't want to be in the way."

Jessica had frowned. "Both Ms. Jones and I would feel more comfortable if you were on site, especially for the first big event. Besides, the guests were impressed by your displays at the library brunch. It would be nice for you to be available to answer questions and chat with them."

When Alexandra had opened her mouth to protest again, Jessica had speared her with an intense gaze.

"I recall in your proposal to Mr. Santos that you mentioned your flowers adding a personal touch that so many companies lacked. Surely, your attendance would reinforce that."

Alexandra had been trapped, and Jessica knew it. When Alexandra had pointed out she'd brought nothing more than a sundress, Jessica had disappeared upstairs and returned with a very large violet bag marked with the silver label of an exclusive boutique Alexandra had used to shop at in her early college days.

"What's this?"

"You mentioned during our tour this had been one of your favorite shops." Jessica had glanced down at Alexandra's T-shirt and jeans, her lips thinning. "Your standard uniform is appropriate for your shop. But I took the liberty of picking up several items in case you were needed for events like these."

Coming from almost anyone else, Alexandra would have taken the comment as an insult. Coming from Jessica, though, it wasn't meant to be rude. It was just fact.

And, Alexandra admitted as she glanced down at the dress she'd selected, after so many years of thrift store finds and secondhand items, she'd felt like a little kid at Christmas as she'd pulled out the luxury clothing. It had been a very long time since she'd worn new garments.

Her favorite had been an off-the-shoulder sage-green gown with a sweetheart neckline and a long, flowing skirt. The slit over one thigh had elevated the dress from elegant to subtly sexy.

She'd set aside the dress, though, when she'd found herself wondering what Grant would think of her in it. Not a professional train of thought, nor a wise one. Daydreaming about Grant would only lead to more confusion and, ultimately, heartache.

The dress she wore now—a white creation with wide straps, a square neck and a fitted top that flared out into a wide skirt with blue swirls that swished about her knees when she walked—had given her a renewed sense of confidence when she'd stationed herself on the deck.

Really, being out here to mingle with Grant's guests was an incredible opportunity for The Flower Bell. She'd even remembered to tuck a few business cards into the pocket of her skirt. The only drawback was that her plan to stay as far away from Grant as possible had disappeared in a puff of smoke.

Right now he stood off to the side talking with a silver-haired couple and a younger, black-haired woman with a bubbly smile. As she'd circulated around the deck, sipping on water with lemon, she'd overheard several of Grant's conversations with his guests. Unlike her father, who had reminded her of an upscale used car salesman with his too-wide smile and overly boisterous laugh, Grant was real, authentic in his communications and genuinely friendly.

His rigidness had disappeared. Now, as he talked with the couple and whom she assumed was their daughter, his smile was like the one she'd glimpsed in his biography picture at the library—genuine and warm.

Apparently, the only person who made Grant uptight and irritable was her.

Jessica walked up.

"The dress suits you."

Alexandra smiled shyly. "Thank you. I haven't worn anything like this in a very long time. I can't wait to wear the green evening gown to the Met gala. I felt like Cinderella when I held it up."

Jessica returned the smile with a tiny twitch of her lips that was most likely her version of a smile. "All you need is a pair of glass slippers."

"I once saw a pair of Christian Louboutin heels that looked like the real-life version of Cinderella's shoes."

"After your work for the Pearson Group, you could afford several pairs of Louboutins."

Jessica wasn't wrong. But there were other things that now took priority. Things like rent and hiring more staff.

"Maybe."

"There's a guest here who would like to meet you."

Jessica gestured for Alexandra to join her as she marched toward a man dressed in a navy polo shirt and tan slacks. As Alexandra passed Grant, she overheard part of his conversation.

"...not sure our fund would be the best fit in that case, Mr. Friedman. Next year might be a better time to look at your finances and whether we would be a good fit."

Alexandra nearly dropped her water glass. Never had David Waldsworth done anything but push when it came to getting his clients to invest. But then so had many other of her father's cronies. They hadn't cared about their clients' personal goals or well-being. Their only interest had been the bottom line.

Yes, Grant had changed. But the qualities she'd admired and loved about him all those years ago, especially his sense of honor and his honesty, hadn't. A frustrated sigh escaped her lips. It would be so much easier to keep her heart distant if he had turned into a monstrous ogre.

She pasted a smile on her face as she stopped next to Jessica.

"Alexandra, this is Dan Perri. He and his wife were asking about the flower arrangements."

Dan gave her a quick smile. With silver threads streaking through his dark hair, and round glasses perched on the edge of a beak-like nose, he struck her as an administrative type and not someone who noticed flowers often.

"Kimberly wanted to walk off with the arrangement at the greeting table at brunch yesterday. It was striking."

Alexandra's lips relaxed into a genuine smile. "Thank you, Mr. Perri. That's very kind."

"I haven't heard of The Flower Bell. Do you do other events like this?"

A frisson of excitement leaped inside her belly. "I do. We've been open officially for six months and are just now getting the word out."

Dan cast an appreciative eye over the tables. "This is certainly a good way to do it. Our company is looking for a new florist for the holiday season. We usually host three or four events between Halloween and New Year's. Would you be available for something like that?"

Ten minutes later she'd handed out three business

cards and tentatively booked an anniversary dinner for July. Riding an emotional high, she nearly ran into a woman barreling out of the house.

"I'm sorry, I…" Alexandra's voice trailed off as she took in the woman's red-rimmed eyes and mascara-streaked cheeks.

"Are you all right?"

The woman sniffed and rubbed her nose. Dressed in a flowing blue-and-white-striped dress, she wore her brown hair wound into a chignon that could have passed for a work of art with its intricate curls and twists. She couldn't have been more than three or four years older than Alexandra.

"I will be as soon as I leave this damned house."

The woman's voice rose to a high pitch at the end. Alexandra glanced around. A couple of guests at the nearest table were watching the scene play out with undisguised curiosity. One of the investment managers Jessica had introduced her to just before the guests had arrived—Steve something—glanced at the woman with a look of petrified horror. Apparently, he could face down stock markets, but not a crying woman. Neither Laura nor Jessica were anywhere to be seen, and Grant was still talking with the Friedmans.

"How about I take you inside?" Alexandra suggested gently.

The woman took a step back.

"Who are you? I don't even know you."

The smell of alcohol hit Alexandra square in the face. Whatever had been happening the past hour, the woman had been using wine to deal with it.

"My name is Alexandra and I'm the florist for the Pearson Group." Even though the woman was glaring at her, something in her manner told Alexandra there was more going on than just a guest who had had too much to drink. "I always feel better being away from a crowd when I'm upset."

The woman blinked, her eyes sliding over Alexandra's shoulder to take in the crowded deck. Red suffused her cheeks as she ducked her head and mumbled, "Okay."

Alexandra gently but firmly grasped the woman by the elbow and led her through the kitchen. Her friend Pamela glanced up from one of the stoves and frowned. Her short brown hair had been pinned beneath her chef's cap, her hands moving with lightning speed even as she mouthed, "Are you okay?" Alexandra nodded and Pamela returned to her work, barking orders at her three chefs, their cooking and plating creating background noise that covered up the woman bursting into sobs as Alexandra maneuvered her into the breakfast nook just off the kitchen. Alexandra sat her down at the table, where she buried her face in her hands.

"I'm sorry. You must think the worst of me."

Alexandra eased into a chair across from her.

"Not really. More curious and worried."

The woman looked up and swiped her cheeks, smearing her mascara farther.

"My husband told me we were coming to the Hamptons for the week. I thought it was for our anniversary. It wasn't until we got here that I realized it was a work thing."

She spat out the word *work* with such animosity that Alexandra guessed this had been an ongoing battle between the woman and her husband.

"That had to be disappointing."

The woman sniffed. "You have no idea. I've been trying to get us into counseling for a year. All he does is focus on how much money he can make. He's become obsessed. He doesn't pay any attention to me or our son."

Alexandra stood and poured the woman a glass of water from the sideboard. She handed it to her, along with a napkin, and resisted giving the woman a hug. How many times had she heard her two stepmothers utter the same sentiment? Her father had ignored them, and he had ignored her. Too many times David hadn't bothered to show up to her piano recitals or polo matches, activities he'd pushed her to do to show off his accomplished daughter but didn't bother to see how hard she'd thrown herself into them, all in an effort to please a man who couldn't be pleased.

"What has he said about counseling?"

Beneath the harshness of the woman's laugh lurked a pain Alexandra was all too familiar with.

"Not enough time. Never enough time when there's money to be made."

Alexandra hesitated. She'd known the woman for all of five minutes. She certainly wasn't a good person to give relationship advice, and perhaps the woman wanted nothing more than to vent. But the circumstances she was describing sounded all too familiar. What if she stayed, seduced by the lifestyle her husband provided or by a futile hope that things might improve?

"Have you thought about leaving?" she finally asked.

The woman slowly shook her head. "I mean, I have. But the worst part is I love him. And he wasn't always like this."

"What changed?"

"A friend of his lost everything in an investment scam two years ago."

Alexandra looked away as nausea crawled up her throat.

"I'm sorry."

"Thank you." The woman plucked at the tablecloth. "When I say everything, I mean everything. His wife left him, he lost his job, the house. Now Harry's become obsessed at making sure we have 'enough.' Which I guess I should appreciate. I just miss my husband." She blew her nose, looked up and grimaced at the gilded mirror on the far wall. "I'm a mess, aren't I?"

Alexandra smiled reassuringly. "Nothing a splash of cold water won't fix. Your hair is stunning, by the way."

The woman laughed again, this time softer with a hint of self-deprecation.

"I thought Harry was taking me out to dinner for our anniversary. I spent two hours getting ready." She shook her head as she stood. "I don't know. Maybe I just need to accept things the way they are."

"No."

The woman looked just as shocked as Alexandra felt at her emphatic response.

"I mean…it sounds like you love him. I once gave up on something I should have fought for." Her voice dimmed as she recalled Grant's brilliant smile on the deck. A smile she would most likely never see aimed in her direction again. "I've regretted it almost every day since."

She blinked away her memories and refocused on the woman standing next to her, gripping the back of her chair like it was a lifeline.

"If you think your marriage is worth saving, don't give up."

The woman stared at her for a long moment before offering her a shy smile.

"Thank you... Alexandra?"

"Yes. Alexandra Moss."

"I'm Lucy Hill." Lucy cocked her head to one side. "You didn't used to be Alexandra Waldsworth, did you?"

The floor opened beneath her as her breath rushed out of her chest.

"Um... I..."

Lucy waved a manicured hand. "I'm sorry, that was crass. I knew your stepmother Susan back in the day, and I think I attended one of the Labor Day parties your family used to throw at the end of the summer."

At least Lucy wasn't screaming or throwing things at her, so that was an improvement over what Alexandra had envisioned happening when she ran into someone from her past.

"I used to be, yes."

Lucy leaned down and laid a comforting hand over hers.

"You don't have to be nervous. The majority of the people who knew your father knew you and your stepbrother weren't to blame."

Alexandra's eyes widened.

"What?"

"Your father had a reputation. Most people felt sorry for you and Finley. I'm glad to see you landed on your own feet and are doing so well." She uttered another self-conscious laugh. "Well, aside from having to deal with a tipsy wife experiencing a marriage crisis. I'm going to clean up before anyone else sees me looking like a raccoon."

Lucy disappeared out into the hall before Alexandra could respond and she sat back in her chair, floored by the exchange she'd just had. Her own fears and guilt over what had happened had haunted her for years, colored so many interactions. When the agent had denied her the storefront in Greenwich Village and made it so difficult to rent a quality property, she'd accepted that her worst suspicions had been true; people blamed her for what her father had done.

But now, with Lucy's kind words lingering in the air, she didn't know what to think.

"Miss Moss?"

Alexandra looked up to see a man in his early forties with thinning blond hair and a morose expression on his narrow face standing in the door.

"Yes?"

"I'm Harry Hill."

Oh, Lord. How had she gotten sucked into the middle of a marriage mess?

"It's nice to meet you, Mr. Hill." She stood and held out her hand. "I think your wife stepped out to use the restroom."

"I heard everything." Harry shoved a hand through his hair. "I'm an idiot."

"Not an idiot," Alexandra hurried to reassure him. "Just…perhaps misguided?"

"A misguided idiot." Harry blew out a harsh breath. Even though Alexandra wanted to escape as quickly as possible—she was a florist, not a marriage counselor—she couldn't help but feel for the couple. Unlike her father and his parade of women, they seemed to truly care about each other. They just hadn't communicated in what seemed like a very long time.

"I didn't even remember that tonight's our anniversary. Not just any anniversary, but our ten-year anniversary." He grimaced. "How does someone forget something like that? I didn't even buy her flowers."

Alexandra started to smile.

"Mr. Hill, I might be able to help you. That is, if you—"

"Yes!" Harry cut her off. "Please, anything. I don't want to lose my wife."

"Follow me."

As they stepped out into the hall, a floorboard creaked. Alexandra looked over her shoulder, expecting to see Lucy coming out of the bathroom. But the hall was thankfully empty. If Lucy could stay in the bathroom for just a few more minutes, she had the perfect solution to help Harry begin the journey of earning his wife's forgiveness.

CHAPTER TEN

GRANT PAUSED IN the doorway of the kitchen, his eyes raking over Alexandra as she tucked a flower into a bouquet. Her dark hair had been pulled up into a ponytail on top of her head. The style left her face bare to his appreciative gaze. She bit down on her lower lip as she turned the flower a fraction and stepped back. To him, the arrangement looked stunning, just like everything else she'd done over the past few days. But watching her work, her attention to detail, showed him that while his initial reasons for hiring her might have been for entirely personal and vengeful purposes, he'd done the right thing. Alexandra was truly a gifted florist.

It had been seeing her talent on display inside the library's elegant Astor Hall and hearing from the guests how much they'd enjoyed the accompanying note cards explaining the meaning behind the flowers selected, complete with a handwritten note thanking them for coming, that had sent him to the Hamptons early. Like a moth to a flame, he hadn't been able to stay away. Not when he'd seen the effort she had put into helping him achieve his desires.

And then there had been her passionate defense of him last night in the kitchen, a secret he had never intended to divulge but that had nonetheless broken free from the cage he'd kept it in all these years. He'd never even told his mother his darkest desire, to use his wealth to eradicate the cartel that had ripped so much from them. Finding out a rival group had taken care of the problem once and for all had been both a relief and a regret. Relief that he wouldn't have to face a decision that would have most likely resulted in bribery, injury and perhaps even death. Regret that he hadn't been able to deliver the ultimate revenge.

Revenge.

That ugly word reared its head as he watched Alexandra circle the counter and examine the flowers from another angle. He had hired Alexandra to rub his wealth and success in her face. If she had picked up on that, she hadn't given any indication. No, she'd done something much worse; she'd poured herself into her work and made him look far better than he was.

Light from the Edison-style bulbs hanging from the ceiling cast a golden hue over her skin. Even though he had instructed Jessica to act as if the clothes she'd picked up in New York were from her, it had pleased him, to a concerning degree, when Alexandra had stepped out in the white-and-blue dress. Not only had she looked stunning, but also seeing something he had picked out on her body had made him feel like she was his.

When he'd first sent the clothing order to Jessica, he'd told himself it was because Alexandra flitting around the Hamptons house in her jeans and T-shirt wouldn't be appropriate. But there had been a part of him that had wanted to do something nice for her, something to assuage his guilt at his own desire to show her up and flaunt his success when she had repeatedly done nothing but go above and beyond in helping him wow his guests. She had always enjoyed dressing up in the past. Judging by the clothes he'd glimpsed hanging up in the little recess in her tiny apartment, not to mention her attractive but threadbare outfit she'd worn to his office when she'd come to deliver her proposal, she didn't have the money to spend on things like that anymore.

When he'd spied her running her hand over the skirt of her dress, a tiny smile playing about her lips, the jolt of satisfaction he'd experienced had bordered on the ridiculous. Unfortunately, the appreciative glances thrown her way by some of his guests had elicited a jealousy he'd managed to temper as he'd dived deeper into the various investment funds and options the Pearson Group was offering its clients.

But it had been hard. Hard to keep his attention centered on the conversations that could make or break his career instead of grabbing Alexandra, hauling her inside and finishing what they had started in the kitchen last night.

When he'd seen Lucy Hill rush out of the house, he'd been prepared for a battle. He knew through the gossip vine that wound its way through New York's upper crust that the Hills had been having marital problems. But Harry had also been funneling millions of dollars into various funds. Not inviting him would have been foolish.

Still, with Jessica inside dealing with the caterers, Grant had been prepared for the worst when he'd seen Lucy's red eyes and ruined makeup. He'd been concerned when he saw Alexandra walk Lucy back into the house, but it had taken a while to wrap up his conversation with the Friedmans without seeming rude. By the time he'd made it inside, it had taken several minutes to track the women down. He'd found them in the breakfast nook just as Alexandra had said, *I once gave up on something I should have fought for...*

He knew, deep down, that she had been talking about them. He'd wanted to burst into the nook and ask for—no, demand—an answer. But he'd hung back, partly out of respect for Lucy and her crisis, and partly because he wasn't sure he was ready to hear Alexandra's response. He'd been debating whether to go in after Lucy had gone to clean up when Harry had entered the fray so he'd hung back, just around the corner, then followed them to the pantry where Alexandra had pulled a bouquet from the spare fridge and told Harry to take Lucy out to a small restaurant up the beach.

"Open until midnight, and the seaside tables are perfect for an anniversary," she'd said with a kind smile.

That smile had slammed into his chest with a force that had almost stolen the breath from his lungs. He could acknowledge now that his so-called quest for revenge had been nothing but a cover. What he'd wanted—no, *needed*—was to understand what had happened all those years ago. How someone with a kind smile and generous heart could have such a cruel side.

Judging by the look of ecstatic happiness on Lucy Hill's face when she and Harry had come back out on the deck ten minutes later and expressed regrets that they weren't staying for the rest of the dinner, Alexandra's kindness had once again helped someone in need.

He had to ask her, he decided as he stepped into the kitchen. He had to know what truly happened, how the woman who gave up a bouquet she had worked so hard on to a man who had forgotten his anniversary and was on the verge of losing his marriage could say such vindictive and hurtful things to someone she had claimed to love.

"It's almost midnight."

Alexandra jumped, one hand flying to her chest as she whirled about.

"You have to stop doing that," she said with a smile that took the sting out of her words.

"Still working?"

She glanced back at the flowers. "Yeah, I needed one more arrangement for the guest rooms tomorrow."

"Because you gave the one you'd prepared to Harry Hill."

Her face clouded for a moment, then cleared as understanding dawned.

"You were out in the hallway, weren't you?" At Grant's nod, she grimaced. "When Jessica asked me to come to the dinner, I didn't think I would end up playing therapist to New York's elite."

"You did more than any three-hundred-dollar-an-hour counselor could have done with those two. They've been having problems for a couple years."

Alexandra looked away.

"Yeah, Lucy mentioned that."

"It wasn't your fault, you know."

Alexandra's head snapped up.

"What?"

"What your father did. It wasn't your fault."

Her throat moved as she swallowed hard.

"I don't…" She sighed and kicked off her white heels before sitting down on a stool with a heavy sigh. "It's hard not to take responsibility. For a long time I didn't pay attention to anything my father did. I just took everything he gave me."

"That's not true." Grant advanced into the kitchen and sat on the stool next to her. "I met you working in the gardens, Alexandra. You weren't just some spoiled, lazy brat. You remembered people's names and helped them out. Do you remember Louis?"

Alexandra smiled. "Yes. He was a dear."

"Do you remember when he sprained his ankle?"

Her face clouded over. "I do. My father wouldn't give the gardening staff sick time."

"And you covered for him. Every time your father wanted to know where he was, you told him Louis was off at the outdoor pool or the docks. He kept his job because of you."

Her smile returned, soft and cautious. "I'm surprised you remember that."

"I do. I remember it all." He reached out and slowly settled his hand over hers. Her sharp intake of breath sent desire bolting through his veins, but he kept his focus on the question he needed to ask. "Which is why I don't understand what happened that summer. Why it ended the way it did."

Silence thickened between them. Alexandra stared at him, hazel eyes wide and glimmering.

"I didn't have a choice, Grant."

Before he could reply, she shook her head.

"That's not true. I had a choice. And I made a choice out of fear."

A hard knot tightened his stomach.

"What are you talking about?"

She breathed in deeply and closed her eyes. The knot

grew heavier. What could have possibly happened that she couldn't even look him in the eye?

"Grant…"

A tear trickled down her cheek. He reached up and brushed it away, then gave in to temptation and cupped her cheek. Her lips parted and she sighed, leaned into his touch.

Desire flooded his body as the knot in his stomach disappeared, replaced by a throbbing need. His harsh exhale echoed in the room like a gunshot. Her eyes flew open. A split second later her eyes darkened as her fingers curled beneath his on the counter.

"Grant."

This time she said his name in a voice roughened by lust. He needed answers, needed to know what had happened all those years ago.

But not now. Right now he needed Alexandra.

It was his last coherent thought as he closed the distance between them and kissed her.

CHAPTER ELEVEN

IT HAD BEEN INEVITABLE, Alexandra realized as Grant's lips pressed against hers and she tangled her fingers in his hair, that this would happen. Somewhere deep inside, no matter how much she'd reminded herself to keep her distance, a part of her had known from the moment she'd laid eyes on him in his office in New York City that they would crash into each other once again. Their love affair had been too passionate, too fiery, too all-consuming, for them to resist each other for long.

He moved with sudden, dizzying speed, lifting her off the stool and pressing her up against the wall. Knowing anyone could walk in at any moment sent a delicious, forbidden bolt of fire through her. He wanted her this badly, craved her as much as she craved him, that it didn't matter. Nothing mattered except feeling him against her again.

Grant's hands closed around her waist and he lifted her up. She followed his lead, their lips never breaking apart as she wrapped her legs around him and pressed her chest fully against his. He groaned and thrust his hips against hers. He swallowed her soft cry as the sensation of his hardness pressed against her core.

"Grant," she whimpered. "Oh, Grant, please."

He wrapped his arms around her, turned and took the back stairs, the steps creaking beneath their combined weight. The last vestige of her rational mind listened for sounds of discovery: a horrified gasp, an exclamation from a guest.

But there was nothing. Nothing but the sound of her heartbeat pounding in her ears as they continued to kiss, to touch, as he walked up the stairs, turned and entered his room, closing the door with a kick.

She was so focused on returning his fevered kisses that it barely registered that she was falling backward until her back hit the mattress. Her eyes flew open as he released her and stepped back. She pushed up on her elbows, barely resisting reaching out to him as fear pierced through her desire.

Had he changed his mind?

"You're so damned beautiful."

The raw hunger in his voice spread through her like wildfire. Emboldened, she pushed up on her elbows and raked him with a fiery, appreciative glance of her own. It wasn't just by design; he truly was magnificent. She'd thought him handsome before but the years had chiseled him from boyish and loving into a dominant leader with a lethal, seductive charm. A charm he leveled at her as he reached down and pulled his shirt over his head in one swift movement.

Moonlight filtered in from the window behind him and backlit his incredible body with silver light. She'd been all too aware of how broad his shoulders had become. But seeing firsthand the muscles rippling across his chest, dusted with dark hair that trailed down below the waistband of his pants, made her mouth dry.

"I can't help but notice you're still fully dressed."

Her head jerked up and she met his amused gaze.
The old her would have blushed and shyly complied
with the unspoken edict. But now…

"I think you should be naked first."

He blinked. "Oh, really?"

She smiled at him, savoring the rise and fall of his
chest as his breathing grew harsh. Harsh because of her.
Because he wanted *her*.

"Yes."

He stared at her, golden brown eyes glittering in the
dark. Had she pushed too far?

His hands drifted down to his belt. Her breath caught
in her chest as he undid the buckle, unzipped his pants
and stepped out of them, revealing black, skintight boxers and firm, muscular legs. Despite the dim light, she
could make out the thickness straining against his boxers.

And then he was removing those, too, revealing himself in all his naked glory. She stared, her lips parting.
Nine years. It had been nine years since she'd seen him
naked; nine years since she'd felt him inside her. Seeing him again, being reminded of the intimacy they had
shared, made her so hot and wet she moved on the bed,
trying to assuage the growing ache between her thighs.

"You look…" She moistened her lips with the tip of
her tongue. "You're incredible, Grant."

The smug smile that crossed his face was both en-
dearing and provoking. She scooted to the edge of the
bed, sat up and reached out before her nerves could get
the better of her. Her fingers closed around his hard
length. His breath hissed out.

"Alexandra."

She looked up at him with a satisfied smile of her own.

"I missed you, Grant."

Her admission surprised both of them. He watched her with an enigmatic gaze that unsettled her. Did he suspect that it wasn't just physical passion spurring her on?

She pushed that disquieting possibility away and lowered her mouth to him. His guttural moan filled the room as she caressed him with her lips and tongue. Her other hand drifted up to settle on his thigh, her fingertips caressing the hardened muscle and coarse hair dusting his skin. His fingers tangled in her hair as he groaned her name.

"*Deus*, Alexandra."

His body tensed, his muscles hardening even more as she brought him to the edge. She savored the power she wielded with her touch as the scent of him, smoky cedar and rich amber, enveloped her in the seductive hold of the past. A seduction made even more potent by the intoxication of the unknown, the unexplored possibilities of the night that lay before them. No longer did the past nine years seem like a gaping wound between them. Now it was exciting, reuniting with a lover who knew her body better than anyone else while discovering new things.

Things like her newfound confidence as her fingers glided up and down his thigh in time with her caresses on the base of his hardness, the sharp inhalation as his fingers tightened even more. He never would have touched her like that before, so possessively. He'd always tried to protect her, keep her safe. At the time, she'd loved it. But now, feeling him respond to her hunger and treat her like an equal, filled her with a fervor that rose into a fever pitch and made her skin blaze with heat.

"Enough."

Grant reached down and hauled her to her feet. His mouth crushed hers in a greedy kiss, one that lasted for only a second but imprinted itself on her soul. Then he stepped back, his hands pulling her dress over her head, fingers deftly unclipping her bra before sliding down and making quick work of her underwear. Gone was the suave, controlled billionaire. In his place was a man possessed by desire, overcome by his need for her.

As his hands glided over her skin, a thought flickered through her mind.

How could I have let this go? How could I have not fought for him?

And then he stepped back even more, eyes raking over her nude body with avaricious need. Cool air whispered over her skin, a welcome balm for the fervor burning through her body.

Focus on now. Make this night worth it. For both of you.

With that commitment echoing in her mind, she raised her chin, sucked in a deep breath and stepped forward. He watched her, jaw clenched tight, arms rigid at his sides. Slowly, she brought her hands up and looped them around his neck, keeping a sliver of moonlight between their bodies as she waited, heightening the anticipation.

Then, ever so slowly, she rose onto her toes and pressed a featherlight kiss on his lips.

"I want you."

Grant stared down at Alexandra. When had she turned into such a captivating temptress? Their lovemaking before had been sweet, tender and gentle. Never had she been this bold, this daring. He'd loved her that summer, introducing her to physical pleasure and worshipping her body.

But this, this was something familiar and yet entirely new. Something he couldn't have turned away from him even if he'd wanted to. He needed not just the physical release of sex but the connection of unifying with a past lover who had known him, all of him.

An unwelcome thought infiltrated the haze of his desire. What if this bewitching side of her had developed over the years as she'd explored her sexuality with other lovers? The thought made him see red as jealousy wrapped around his heart and squeezed. Unreasonable, given that he'd had two lovers of his own since they'd parted. But he could barely stomach it. The image of another man touching her body made him want to hunt the phantom down and wrap his hands around his throat.

Dimly, he became aware of Alexandra's hold around his neck loosening. The boldness in her eyes flickered, uncertainty creeping across her face. His hands came up, fingertips gliding over her hips and grazing the sides of her breasts with a touch as light as butterfly wings. A touch that reassured her that he wanted her even as it reassured him that, no matter what had happened, Alexandra was with him now. If there was a time for revisiting the past, it would be later. Not now, not when he had her naked in his arms.

He reveled in the parting of her lips, her eyes widening, her breath quickening as his hands moved around to her back, still caressing with the barest of touches. His desire swelled, the sensitive tip grazing her stomach.

"I want you, too."

His hands grasped her about the waist. She gasped,

her hands bracing on his shoulders as he lifted her up and draped her across the bed. She reached for him, but he stepped back, a slight smile on his lips to show her he wasn't going far. But given how she'd nearly made him lose control, he had to return the favor before he completely surrendered.

The moonlight lit up his bed and made Alexandra's skin glow. Her hair lay in a thick mahogany curtain beneath her. Her breasts, so often hidden beneath those damned T-shirts, were round and fuller than they had been. She'd grown into her womanhood, her body filling out with seductive curves that begged for his hands to explore every inch. He moved to the bed, watching as her breasts rose and fell, her nipples tightening into points.

Slowly, he climbed up on the bed, caging her between his arms but keeping distance between them. He leaned down and pressed a kiss to the swell of one breast. She arched up, silently pleading for a firmer touch. He resisted the temptation to rush. He'd waited nine years for this moment. He would be damned if he didn't enjoy all of it.

He continued his kisses over her breasts, kissing and gently nipping all around her nipples. Her body shifted, hands fisting in the silk sheets as she made tiny sounds of frustration.

"Please, Grant."

He raised his head and waited for her to look at him before giving her a wolfish smile.

"Since you said please."

Before she could utter a retort, he leaned down and sucked one hardened nipple into his mouth. She cried out and arched off the bed.

"Grant!"

He made love to her breasts with his mouth, still holding himself above her, not trusting himself to press his naked body against hers until he was ready to slide into her welcoming heat. He kissed and sucked and nibbled his way down between the valley of her breasts, across the slight swell of her stomach and down to her thighs.

"Grant…"

This time her voice held a hint of doubt. He looked up and held her gaze with his.

"I won't if you don't want me to, Alexandra. But," he added as he brought one finger up and slid it along the delicate seam of her wet folds, "I hope you want me to kiss you as much as I want to taste you."

The silver moonlight revealed the delicate pink that crept over her cheeks even as she smiled, shyness tangling with that audacious new boldness. Seeing a glimpse of her old demureness reassured him. He had changed. Alexandra had changed. But there were still threads of who they used to be beneath the surface. He still didn't have the answers, would probably never know what had happened all those years ago.

But some of it had been real. And right now that was enough.

One hand came up and cupped his cheek. The soft touch traveled through him, barreling through his defenses and seizing hold of whatever emotions had been reawakened the night of her attack.

Emotions better left under lock and key if he wanted to avoid getting hurt again.

"Yes, Grant."

His hands clenched on her hips like a vise, pinning

her in place as he lowered his head to her most vulnerable place. His first kiss elicited a moan that he hoped wasn't heard by the guests, although a reckless part of him didn't care if it was. Jessica and his housekeeper Sara were available if the guests needed anything, giving him the incredible opportunity of forgetting everything but the woman beneath him.

His fleeting thought of concerned guests disappeared as he was filled with the scent of her, the sweet taste of her desire for him. He trailed his lips over her most sensitive skin, used his tongue to bring her to the height of pleasure as she writhed beneath him, her fingers moving through his hair, over his face, grasping at his shoulders as she gasped and whimpered and begged.

He didn't relent, not even as her hips started to pump against his mouth, her cries growing as her thighs clenched around his head. She grabbed a pillow and pressed it over her face just as her back bowed off the bed and her body shuddered with a powerful release.

As she slowly relaxed back into the welcoming embrace of the bed, he reached into his end table and said a silent prayer of thanks when his fingers brushed against a condom packet. He ripped open the package, sheathed himself and then lowered himself onto the bed, pulling the pillow off her face as he pressed his naked body flush against hers. Her molten core cradled his thickness, her heat nearly undoing him.

"I need to be inside you."

Her eyes were glazed, her lips still parted, but as soon as she nodded, he pressed inside her slowly, savoring the sensation of her tight wetness closing around him.

At last, when he was fully sheathed inside her, he

leaned down and covered her mouth with his. It was a kiss that brought him home, back to the past but also to the present, with the woman he'd never been able to fully eradicate from his heart beneath him, surrounding him, drawing him deeper into a passionate web he'd once thought himself free of.

As he began to move, slowly at first and then fiercer, deeper, capturing her cries with his lips as they both rode the rising wave of pleasure toward its peak, he wondered why he had ever wanted to be free.

She burst around him, crying out into his mouth as her nails sank into his back, her body matching his in perfect rhythm. He followed a moment later, sinking so deeply into her warm and willing body he never wanted to let go.

But he rolled off her, not wanting to crush her into the bed. When she started to inch her way toward the edge, he flung an arm around her waist and dragged her close.

"Where do you think you're going?"

She turned to look at him, her eyes surprisingly opaque. Once she'd been an open book. He could tell her every thought.

Although, he remembered as his ardor cooled, he thought he had.

"I… This was incredible."

"Yes."

Amusement flashed in her eyes and softened her face.

"Yes. I just wasn't sure… I know we're not…"

How easy it would be to use this moment, to turn the tables and reject her the way she had him. Remind her of the difference in their stations in life and thank her for a pleasant evening before asking her to leave.

The first day she had walked into his office, he might have been able to do it. But now, after everything that had transpired between them in just a couple weeks, and with the evidence mounting that there was much more to the story of their breakup, he couldn't. Couldn't deliver such cruelty and heartbreak for the sake of avenging his wounded pride.

"The choice to leave is yours."

She stared at him for a moment longer. He didn't know what he wanted more: for her to stay and for them to indulge in their rediscovered passion, or for her to leave and give him a chance to regroup before morning dawned. To prepare himself for whatever bombshell she had to drop.

The smile she gave him was forced, insincere.

"I should go."

Disappointment chased away the warmth left over from their lovemaking. But he didn't stop her as she rolled out of bed. He watched as she moved about the room, pulling on her clothes with quick movements, rushing to get away from him. The weak part of him that had felt something more as they'd made love urged him to ask her to stay. Reality and pride silenced his foolishness as his anger resurfaced. If she wanted to run away instead of giving him the answers he deserved, fine.

She was nearly at the door, her back to him, when she paused.

Stay.

The word rose to the tip of his tongue, nearly fell from his lips.

But he managed to stay silent. A moment later she turned the knob and disappeared, closing the door softly behind her.

CHAPTER TWELVE

ALEXANDRA'S GAZE FLITTED from one flower arrangement to the next, visually checking for any sign of sagging blooms or browning leaves. But everything looked perfect.

She closed the refrigerator door with a sigh. She should be satisfied, but all she could think was this left her with absolutely nothing to do on her last full day in the Hamptons. Tomorrow would end with a luncheon before everyone headed back to their respective homes. Some lived in New York City, but others had traveled from Washington, D.C., the Carolinas and even from Kansas City, in the case of one real estate tycoon. They would all return for the final event, the gala at the Met for over two hundred prospective clients and influential members of the New York financial community. Thankfully, it wasn't until next Saturday, giving her a week to decompress from what had turned out to be an emotionally trying few days.

She'd seen Grant every day since she'd fled his bedroom the night they'd made love, but aside from greeting him with a "Hello, Mr. Santos," she'd kept her distance. He hadn't approached her, either, had barely even glanced in her direction.

And why would he? She'd once again fled rather than faced up to the sins of her past. She'd wanted nothing more than to stay in his arms that night and tell him every horrible detail. Yet, she hadn't been able to move past the very real possibility that he would look at her in disgust before telling her to get out. He'd survived fleeing a drug cartel, living in a postage stamp-size apartment and working himself to the bone to provide for his mother as he'd worked toward his dream. If he had been in her shoes all those years ago, he would have found a way for them to stay together. If she did tell him the truth, how could he see her as anything but weak?

As much as it had hurt, leaving him that night had been the right thing to do. It had saved them both the anger and recriminations that would come with such a conversation. And it had allowed her to hold on to the memory of him pulling her close just after their love-making. A moment she never thought to have again, a gift worth preserving.

She moved upstairs into the kitchen where Pamela and her crew were cooking up breakfast. Part of her wanted to talk to her friend, to tell her everything and get her opinion. But if Pamela knew who she really was, knew about her past, she'd never said anything. She told herself she didn't want to burden her friend, not after Pamela had already risked her own job giving Alexandra the information she had.

But truthfully, she acknowledged as she grabbed a muffin and waved at Pamela before moving over to one of several state-of-the-art coffee machines, most of it was fear. She didn't want to confide in anyone else, to risk having someone else turn away from her because of her past.

Today had been described on the itinerary as a down day for guests with suggestions on the various sights and favored treasures of the Hamptons. Pamela and her team would keep a steady stream of snacks and light meals going throughout the day. She'd passed Jessica working in the library, Laura spending time with one of the guests in the sunroom. Most of the other guests had made use of the limos that were on standby to take them wherever they wanted to go. The other Pearson executives had flown back to New York for the day.

Leaving her with an entire day of nothing but stewing in her own thoughts.

She grabbed a cup of coffee and walked out onto the back deck. She'd been up since sunrise, putting the final touches on the arrangements for tomorrow's lunch. Most nights she'd collapsed into bed just after dusk had settled over the ocean. Between the flowers for the guest rooms and the various events Grant had hosted, plus updating her website and organizing the flurry of new orders starting to trickle in, she hadn't had time for anything but work.

She settled onto a lounge chair and pulled out her phone. No new emails. She'd blocked off orders through the gala, but a few had come in for the week after. A few taps and confirmation emails were sent. She'd scheduled social media posts through the week. And her landlord had actually come through on the electricity.

When was the last time she'd had an entire day to do nothing?

Years, she thought as she sipped her coffee. Jessica had forwarded her a copy of the guest itinerary. Maybe she could visit one of the farms or parks…

Her thoughts trailed off as movement caught her eye.

She turned just in time to see Grant walk into the yard through a side gate. Her jaw dropped. A black bathing suit clung to his muscular thighs, and the white T-shirt he'd pulled on did little in the way of coverage. No, it actually did the opposite and clung to every ridge of his impressive chest. His dark hair curled in wet tangles that she wanted to reach out and brush back from his forehead.

He glanced back over his shoulder at the ocean. Perhaps he hadn't seen her yet. If she could get up fast enough and slip back inside the house, then he wouldn't catch her ogling him like a—

"Good morning."

His deep voice rumbled through her.

"Good morning, Mr. Santos."

He arched a brow as he drew closer and settled into the lounge chair next to her. She kept her gaze trained on the waves of the Atlantic.

"Don't you think *Mr. Santos* is a little formal?"

"It's what you asked me to call you. As my boss."

"That was before you were naked in my bed."

Her head whipped around to make sure no one was listening. When she looked back at Grant, it was to see him watching her with a teasing glint in his brown eyes that belied the seriousness of his expression.

"I've been calling you Mr. Santos all week," she pointed out, her hands wrapping around the coffee mug as she focused on the heat seeping from the porcelain instead of the remembered heat of their night together.

"In public, yes."

She could feel him watching her, waiting for her to say something. She kept her lips pressed firmly together.

"You've been avoiding me."

"You haven't exactly been seeking me out," she replied.

"I am now. We're going to a hydrangea farm."

Not what she had expected. Panic fluttered in her stomach even as a warm thrill shot through her veins at the prospect of spending more time with him. Part of her wondered what scheme he had up his sleeve. But she'd also never been to a hydrangea farm. The big round blooms were a fixture in many yards, but few florists used them in arrangements.

"What if I say no?"

Grant leaned in, the scent of salt mingling with his natural earthy scent.

"You won't. Because even right now you're envisioning rows upon rows of hydrangea blooms. You can't resist."

She barely stopped herself from swaying toward him. He was right. But it wasn't just the enticement of visiting the farm. No, even though she'd been avoiding him all week, suddenly she wanted nothing more than to spend the day with him. Perhaps the last day she'd have, she realized. There would be no reason for them to see each other over the next week. She would deliver the flowers to the Met on Saturday afternoon and then...

Nothing. She and Grant would part ways. He would become a part of the upper echelons of Manhattan society and she would return to her shop.

"Only because you're taking me to a flower farm."

His smile flashed white against his tan skin, an irritatingly satisfied smirk.

"Be ready in fifteen minutes out front."

Alexandra walked out the front door at fifteen minutes on the dot, wearing an indigo wrap dress that stopped just above her knee topped with a loose white shirt knotted at the waist. A straw hat with a white band shaded her face. After their evening together, and the days spent dancing around the growing tension between them, he found himself both relieved and gratified that she had once again worn one of the outfits he'd picked.

Of all the clothing he'd selected, there had been one that had stood out from the rest—an evening gown, a green creation with a full skirt that had made him think of leaves dancing in a summer breeze. He'd told himself the purchase was so she would represent the Pearson Group well at the Met gala, that his guests would see he had selected the best, and ignored the images playing on repeat in his head of sliding his fingers beneath the straps wrapped around her arms, sliding the gown down her lithe body...

An image that, if they could talk, if she would tell him what had happened in the library nine years ago, could become reality.

His chest clenched. He'd kept his distance all week, vacillating between anger and something that resembled the grief he'd experienced in the immediate aftermath of their breakup. But the more he thought of the pain he'd seen in Alexandra's face that night, the fear in her eyes, and the more he'd revisited her comments about her father, the more he'd known he needed to stop letting his own fears keep him from pursuing the truth.

Alexandra took one look at the cherry-red convertible and smiled. A big smile that made her eyes crinkle at the corners.

"You remembered."

"I did."

David had gifted her a red convertible for her nineteenth birthday. Not out of any paternal love but because it had given him the opportunity to show off his wealth that summer. He had encouraged Alexandra, if she wasn't taking the limo somewhere, to drive the convertible. Alexandra and Grant had made the most of it, driving up and down the coast at all hours of the night after he'd gotten off work, parking on the beach and listening to music as they'd lain on the hood and gazed up at the stars.

And once they'd given in to temptation, they'd made love in the backseat more times than he could count.

With the memory of Alexandra splayed across his lap, her naked body rising and falling above him as she'd ridden him to exquisite release, he started the car and drove off down the lane.

The farm was an hour's drive east of Billionaire's Lane. Soft music played as an amiable silence settled between them. Alexandra spent most of the ride gazing out at the summer homes and ocean views. He resisted the urge to push her for answers. He'd been fast-tracking so much of his life the past nine years, always focused on the goal of more money, that he'd stopped enjoying the little things like a ride along the coast.

They were five miles outside East Hampton when a wooden sign advertised the aptly named Hydrangea Farm. As Grant steered the convertible down a tree-lined gravel driveway, he watched Alexandra out of the corner of his eye.

"Oh!"

A white farmhouse with a long front porch greeted them, along with another sign with arrows pointing guests off to areas like the gift shop, coffee shop and beehives. But Alexandra wasn't looking at that. Her attention was riveted to the field off to the side.

Rows upon rows of towering hydrangea bushes covered the fields. Some of the blooms were so thick the branches bowed down to the ground, showering the green grass with petals in various shades of pinks, creams and blues. Ash trees grew here and there among the bushes, creating welcoming pockets of shade as the sun climbed higher in the sky.

"Grant," Alexandra breathed. "This is incredible."

She turned to him, her smile even wider than when she'd seen the car. For something as simple as bringing her to a flower farm. How had he ever thought her spoiled and selfish? How could he have been blind to the fact that something else had obviously been going on behind the scenes when she'd broken up with him?

They parked the car and Alexandra took off toward the fields. He quickened his pace to follow her before she disappeared among the flowering bushes.

At this hour of the morning, the farm was mostly empty, save for the gentle buzzing of bees as they flew from bloom to bloom. Alexandra mimicked them, flitting from bush to bush.

"This is a Golden Crane Hydrangea!" she cried, cupping a bunch of white flowers in her hand and closing her eyes as she inhaled. "You have to smell this. They're unlike any other hydrangea."

Grant followed her directions and lowered his head, pleasantly surprised by the jasmine-like scent.

"They should sell perfume."

Alexandra shook her head.

"It wouldn't be the same." She spread her arms wide and turned about in a circle. "This is just incredible."

He watched, entranced by the sheer happiness radiating from her smile. He'd seen her like this before, so many times over their summer together.

"What happened, Alexandra?"

The smile disappeared from her face. He wanted to make it reappear, to pretend like they could just move forward and never discuss what had happened.

But he needed to know. He had no idea what he was picturing for them or if there would even be a *them* after the gala. He did know, though, that unless they finally crossed this hurdle, whatever had started to grow between them would shrivel and die.

She turned to one of the bushes, her fingers reaching out to gently stroke the petals. He waited.

"The bonfire…" Her voice caught as her head drifted down. "Do you remember the bonfire we went to the week before?"

"Yes."

She'd wanted to go, to see her old school friends. The last thing he'd wanted had been to go to a party with a bunch of rich clowns. But it had meant something to her. She'd hardly had any close friends, so he'd said yes. Delivering a stinging put-down to the idiots who had eyeballed Alexandra like she was a piece of meat had made attending worthwhile. That and Alexandra asking if they could leave early because she wanted to spend time together just the two of them.

"Someone told their parents I was there with you, and they told my father."

The pieces that had always swirled just out of reach started to fall into place with chilling clarity.

"He confronted me the Friday before I broke things off with you." Her tone became flat, her eyes fixed on the flowers. "He told me if I didn't break up with you, and if I told you that he had talked to me, he would make sure you and your mother were sent back to Fortaleza." The tiniest shudder rippled through her. "When I told him you could die if you were sent back, he said that was the idea."

The heat from the sun bore down on him, searing his skin through his shirt.

"What you said in the library…"

"He told me to say those things. He said I had to be as cruel as possible so that you would never want anything to do with me again." A couple of petals drifted down from the bunch she clutched, and she released it as if it was on fire, crossing her arms over her stomach. "He said he could send you back anytime he wanted. That if I ever saw you again, he'd make sure you and your mother were on a plane back to Brazil within twenty-four hours."

Guilt and fury clashed in his chest. He'd known what David was capable of, had seen plenty of evidence of how horrible the man could be. He should have known something was wrong when David had sat in on their breakup with that hideous smile on his lips.

But he'd been so focused on himself, on his own hurt, and thinking that his fears of being inadequate and unequal to someone like Alexandra had been right all along, that he'd missed everything going on behind the scenes.

"That's why you suggested we run away. The night before."

She closed her eyes and nodded. "I… I should have talked to you, Grant. I should have told you what was going on." She opened her eyes and looked at him with such sorrow it nearly killed him. "I'm sorry."

Words he had wanted to hear for nine years. Words that now felt hollow and empty as he realized Alexandra hadn't been at fault, not truly. She'd been at the mercy of a wealthy, powerful man.

"That's not all."

She sucked in a deep, shuddering breath. The buzzing of the bees changed from pleasant to oppressive, the noise matching the roar building in his ears as a dozen scenarios rushed through his mind. What could possibly be worse than what her father had done?

"I…" She pulled her hat off and ran a shaky hand through her hair. "Finn and I weren't close until that fall. Until he had to take me to the hospital."

"The hospital?"

A tear slid down her cheek. "When I miscarried our child."

He'd been punched in the stomach before. The sensation was the same, the world slowing down as all the air escaped his lungs and left him adrift.

" A child?"

Alexandra nodded.

"Three months along. I had no idea. I just assumed the nausea, the exhaustion, all of it was stress. My father was out of the country. I started bleeding and Finn… He took me to the hospital. He held my hand the whole night." A feeble smile crossed her lips. "It was the one good thing that came out of that whole mess. Seeing me like that, hearing what my father did to us, changed Finn."

He would eventually be grateful for the unexpected blessing granted to Alexandra. But right now all he could see was the loss. The loss of a future with the woman he'd loved. The loss of a child he'd never even known existed. More loss, more heartbreak.

Alexandra cleared her throat.

"I should have told you, Grant, and I should have stood up to my father." Her voice cracked. "I've always been so weak—"

"Stop," Grant barked, unable to hear any more. Unable to hear how much he'd let her down. "I…there's a lot to think about."

A shutter dropped over Alexandra's face.

"Of course." She put her hat back on. "I'll just head to the gift shop."

Before he could say another word, she slipped past him and headed back toward the farmhouse.

And he didn't stop her. What could he say? That he had blamed her all these years, had hired her to rub his success in her face because he'd held on to a misplaced grudge instead of seeking her out and finding out what the hell had happened?

He wandered around the hydrangea fields, trying to figure out what he would do, what he should do. By the time he reached the farmhouse, over thirty minutes had passed. He walked into the gift shop, frowning when he didn't see Alexandra.

"Are you Grant Santos?"

Grant turned to see a white-haired woman with a wrinkled face and bright blue eyes smiling at him from behind the counter.

"I am."

"Your friend had to go back to the Hamptons house.

Something about an emergency with the flowers for tomorrow's lunch? She took a taxi back and said she would see you tomorrow."

CHAPTER THIRTEEN

ALEXANDRA WALKED ALONG the beach, her toes digging into the wet sand. The sun had set long ago, but she'd waited until darkness had set in and she'd heard most of the house guests retire to their rooms to slip down the stairs and head toward the beach.

She'd been hiding in her room since she'd gotten back. She'd barely stomached the outrageous taxi bill. But it had been worth the money. At first, she'd committed to waiting for Grant to emerge from the hydrangea fields, to handling whatever mood he was in and either a very awkward silence on the ride home or a full-blown fight.

But as the minutes had ticked by with no sign of him, she hadn't been able to handle it. She'd told him everything, including that they had conceived and lost a child. And all he'd done was stare at her before asking her to stop.

Her throat tightened. She didn't know what she'd expected, but stone-cold silence had not been on her list of possible reactions.

She tilted her head back and looked up at the stars sparkling overhead. How many times had she and Grant lay on the hood of her convertible and stared up at this same sky? How many times had he spread a blanket on the sand, cradling her in his arms as he made love to her?

Part of her still felt guilty that she had allowed her father so much reign over her life. But part of her felt frustrated, too, perhaps even angry. As she'd confessed what had happened, saying it out loud had changed things for her. Yes, she'd been weak. Yes, she should have talked to Grant. But she'd done what she'd done because she had been trying to protect Grant and his mother. Could he not see that she had broken up with him because she loved him? Because loving him and not having him in her life was infinitely preferable to the dangers he would have faced if he had been sent back because she'd risked it all by dragging him to a stupid party?

She stopped at the pier jutting out of the water that marked the end of Grant's beachside property. Awareness pricked her skin. Turning, she saw a dark shape moving toward her on the beach. She knew, even in the dim light of the moon, who moved in her direction. Could tell by the way he walked, the set of his shoulders, the surety of his gait.

"You shouldn't be out here alone."

"I'm not anymore."

As he drew closer, she saw that he was wearing the same linen shirt and slacks he'd worn to the farm. Her heart ached to reach out and touch him. But she held herself in check. He'd told her to stop, unable to bear the confession he'd asked for. Who knew what he wanted now?

"You left."

"It seemed like the best option."

"No." His sigh was barely audible over the gentle roaring of the waves as they crept up the beach. "No, the best option would have been me responding to you and not acting like a self-absorbed idiot."

She stared at him, unsure of how to respond. Part of her wanted to grasp the ray of hope he offered her. But the other part of her couldn't handle another disappointment. Not after the emotional wringing out her heart had been through as she'd dredged up the past.

He held something up. A blanket, she realized.

"It's been ages since we sat on a beach."

She nodded, her throat tight this time for an entirely different reason. Every time they'd spread out a blanket on the beach in the past, it had been to lose themselves in each other's embrace.

"Would you join me?"

Her mind told her to stay strong, to not give in. Her heart was having none of it. She nodded again and watched as he spread the blanket out over the sand. He sat and reached up, holding out a hand to her. She stared at it for a long moment before slowly accepting it. His fingers closed over hers and guided her down to the blanket.

"I didn't know how to respond back at the farm. I was angry at myself. All these years I knew there was something wrong about what had happened in the library. Not just what you said, but your father being there, too. I knew something was off and I let my stupid pride tell me that you had just played me."

Her heart cracked as her own guilt reared its head. Of course he'd been convinced.

"You protested at first," she pointed out gently. "You told me you didn't believe me."

"But then I did. I gave in and did what I accused you of doing." He reached out, one hand closing over hers and enfolding her fingers in his. "I ran away. Being confronted with the reality of what happened, and then finding out that we…"

Her eyes grew hot. She had cried for days after the miscarriage. It had seemed like the cruelest twist of fate, to first lose Grant and then to lose their child.

"You didn't know, Grant."

"But I did," he said fiercely. "I did know, and I failed you. You and our…our child." Slowly, he reached out and cupped her face just like he had that night in the kitchen. "I failed you, Alexandra, and this morning I failed again. I'm sorry."

His apology lifted a heavy weight from her shoulders. Tears splashed down her cheeks as she brought her hand up to cover his.

"You don't have to apologize, Grant."

"I do. I hurt you, Alexandra. You didn't deserve any of the pain your father brought on you, and certainly none of the pain I've brought into your life."

She turned and placed a kiss in the middle of his palm. His breath hissed out. When he kissed her this time, it was a sweet kiss, tender and reminiscent of the first time he'd kissed her in the gardens. His other hand came up and he cradled her face with a tenderness that made tears prick her eyes. Their first time in his bedroom had been fiery, passionate, a fitting reunion given the years they'd been apart.

But this…this was something more. As his lips trailed over her cheek, down her neck and pressed firmly against the pulse beating in her throat, she knew what had changed, at least for her.

She had finally accepted that she was still in love with Grant Santos. A fact that at one time would have driven her into a melancholy state at not being able to let go of the past. If only she had seen sooner that loving Grant had brought out the best in her. He had been the one to challenge her, to encourage her to step outside of her comfort zone and be strong. Unlike the others in her life, he had never wanted someone to be dependent on him. He had wanted her to be free.

Her hands came up, her fingers tangling in his silky hair as she pressed a kiss to his forehead and his hands dropped to her back, pressing her closer.

I love you.

The words stayed locked in her chest, but she showed him, showed him as she undid the buttons on his shirt and kissed the warm skin of his chest. Showed him as she straddled his lap, laced her fingers behind his head and covered his lips with hers with fearless abandon.

Tonight, with the sea roaring behind them and the barest hint of silver moonlight caressing their skin as it waned, she would show him how she felt. And she would do so without fear of what tomorrow would bring.

His fingers slipped beneath the straps of her dress and eased them down over her shoulders. She smiled against his mouth. Each touch of his fingertips, each soft graze, imprinted itself on her memory. How many times had she lain in bed, remembering their passion from that summer and trying to recall the details that her subsequent heartbreak and trauma had erased? She would not make that mistake again.

Cool, salt-tinted air drifted over her breasts as Grant bared them to his gaze. He leaned forward, placed his head on her chest and breathed in deeply, as if he was inhaling the scent of her. She cradled his head in her hands, pressed him against her chest and cherished the intimate moment before he pulled back and captured one nipple in his mouth. She arched against him. He sucked her into the warm heat of his mouth, kissing and licking and nibbling with expert touches that stoked the fires building inside her body. He repeated the same process on her other breast before he pulled the dress over her head. It left her clad in nothing but her panties, legs spread across his lap as she looked down at him.

He leaned back and smirked up at her.

"What are you waiting for?"

Her answering smile was full of promise. She continued her quest to unbutton his shirt, pulling the material free of the waistband of his pants with slow, measured movements. His smirk disappeared as his eyes grew hot, watching her with an intensity that made her so wet she could barely restrain herself from freeing him from the confines of his pants and sinking down onto his hard length.

But she forced herself to go slow. The first time had been them crashing into each other, years of pain and pent-up passion and longing rolled into one incredible moment of sex.

This, though, was different. The past couple of days, overcoming their first true fight, sharing what had happened all those years ago, had made her feel as light as air. The weight of the burden she'd been carrying had been with her for so long she hadn't even realized how heavy it had become, weighing down her life, her future, everything. Without it, she felt like she could conquer the world.

Or reclaim a lost love.

Slow down.

She steadied her emotions, brought herself back under control. Tonight could be just one night, or it could be the beginning of something more. Whatever it was, she would make it last.

She reached down and grabbed his hands, guiding them to her breasts. His eyes turned molten as he cupped their full weight, his thumbs brushing the sensitive tips. She relished his touch before covering his fingers with her own and pushing them down the curves of her waist, over her hips to her thighs. As his hands settled on her, his fingertips pressing into her flesh, she slipped her hands behind his neck and leaned down. She pressed a kiss to his temple, his cheek, the curve of his ear. Her breasts grazed his chest, eliciting sharp inhales from them both as she continued to explore his face with her lips.

His hands crept up her thighs. One finger traced the sensitive skin beneath the waistband of her panties. Another gently rubbed her most sensitive flesh through the thin, lacy material, making her jump beneath his touch at the electricity that spiraled throughout her body.

"You're so wet for me, Alexandra."

His voice, rough and wondering, wound around her. With another smile she leaned down and kissed him deeply.

"Only you, Grant. Ever."

His eyes widened slightly as the meaning of her words sank in. She didn't wait to hear his reply. Instead, she placed her palms on his chest and pushed him back onto the blanket. She stood above him and slowly, teasingly, slipped her panties off, leaving her naked.

Another breeze whispered over her skin. Shyness

crept in as she gazed down at her one and only lover. She loved her newfound confidence, the strength Grant had always insisted she had possessed. She hadn't fully believed him until she'd had no other choice but to be strong.

That didn't mean she was completely confident in her role of seductress, though, especially standing above him completely nude and vulnerable.

Grant pushed up off the blanket and knelt before her. "You're beautiful, Alexandra."

With that pronouncement he placed his hands on her hips and leaned forward to kiss her between her thighs. She gasped, knees trembling, hands clutching at his shoulders as he parted her folds with his tongue.

"Grant!"

His first strokes were gentle. As the stars spun overhead and the sea rolled ever closer with each wave, his mouth firmed on her. He slid one finger inside her, pulsing in time with his lips and tongue. Pressure built inside her, intensifying and spreading throughout her body with a languid heat that suddenly escalated as he wrapped his mouth around her clitoris. One tender suck and she exploded, crying out as the pressure burst into pinpricks of light that spiraled throughout her body. She would have collapsed if Grant hadn't guided her down with his strong hands, pulling her onto the blanket and tucking her into his side.

She didn't know how long they lay there, her body trembling in the aftermath of her pleasure as Grant's fingers lovingly caressed her back.

"I was supposed to be seducing you," she finally said.

Grant's chuckle reverberated against her cheek.

"You did. I just returned the favor."

She slid one arm over his stomach and snuggled her face into the crook of his shoulder. His hand paused on her back, then slowly resumed moving over her skin.

"The last time we were like this, we were just a couple miles down the beach from here."

The warm glow evaporated. No longer did the sea air feel like a balm to the fever Grant had inspired in her. Now it felt cold and harsh as it whipped sand against her bare skin. She shivered.

"I remember that night."

Grant reached down, captured her chin in his hand and turned her to face him.

"Don't turn away from me."

The words were firm, but his voice was kind, his face gentle.

"I'm not."

"Liar."

Liar. Yes, she had lied about a great many things, but not trusting him with why she lied had been her biggest mistake. If she trusted him now, would he be able to see who she had become and allow her to atone for her past weakness?

"Why didn't you tell me that night what was going on?"

She hit pause on the panic building in her stomach and breathed in deeply. The old her would have turned away, wanting to avoid conflict. But it was a reasonable question. It was uncomfortable to revisit that moment, but he deserved an answer.

"I was scared. Scared that if I didn't break things off you and your mom would be sent back." Her voice caught. "I remembered the night you told me about finding your father's body. My heart broke for you. And then it broke for me, because the thought of you being killed…" She closed her eyes against the image that had given her the strength to deliver her performance in the library the following evening, that of Grant lying on a Brazilian street, his chest red with blood and eyes staring unseeing at the sky overhead. "I should have told you what my father had threatened. But I was worried you would confront him, and he would send you back out of spite."

She opened her eyes to see Grant staring down at her. Did he believe her? Or had the cruel words she'd hurled at him in the library, vicious sentiments that had been festering for the past nine years, done too much damage for him to ever be able to fully trust her?

"I sometimes thought about how you said we should run away. Where we would go."

A small laugh escaped her lips. "Running away. It's what I'm good at."

"Don't say that."

She blinked in surprise.

"What?"

"You rebuilt your entire life after losing everything. You could have quit at any point. You could have given up on The Flower Bell after you were turned down for a lease. You stood up to a damned thief." His arm tightened around her waist. "You have grown into an incredibly strong woman, Alexandra."

She surged forward and kissed him, her hands coming up to frame his face as she pressed her lips against his.

Grant surrendered to his need and hauled Alexandra on top of him. Her naked body seared his chest, her heat seeping through his pants. He sat up, keeping their mouths fused together as he reached between them and fumbled with his belt. Alexandra pushed him back onto the blanket and undid his belt and jeans with deft movements. He reached up, his hands cradling the full weight of her breasts, needing to touch her skin, to feel her and reassure himself that she was here, that she wasn't going to run away. He'd meant every word he said, but his damned pride and insecurities wouldn't let him completely forget.

When will you? When will you let go and free yourself?

The thought disappeared as Alexandra rolled his boxers and pants off and his erection sprang free. She settled between his thighs and ran her tongue over every inch of him. He reached down and grasped one hand in his, enfolding her fingers with his as he submitted to the lust she inspired in him.

Until, that is, he could feel his need building, threatening to undo him.

"Enough."

Before he could grab her, she moved up his body with surprising speed and straddled his hips. His breath caught as she placed the tip of his hardness against her wet heat. Knowing that he had been her first and only made the moment all the more potent as she slowly slid down, losing himself in the pleasure as she surrounded him with her silky tightness.

She rode him, then, dark hair falling over her shoulders as she moved above him, hands braced on his chest. He grabbed her hips, guided the building tempo as they thrust against each other. Her fingernails dug into his chest as her mouth rounded into an O and her head dropped back.

"Grant… I'm… Oh, God!"

He knew the moment her orgasm rolled through her, felt her clench around him as she cried out. Seeing her release, feeling her come around him, sent him over the edge with her, continuing to thrust until she collapsed onto his chest.

Unlike their first night of lovemaking, she didn't get up. Instead, she curled into his embrace and once more pressed her face into the crook of his shoulder. He reached over and grabbed the extra length of blanket, pulling it up and over. It barely covered both of them, but it provided enough coverage against the dropping temperatures.

He waited until he heard her breathing slow before he glanced down at her face. In the dim light of the moon she looked peaceful and so beautiful it made his chest ache.

It hadn't just been what sounded like genuine heartbreak in her voice that had caught his attention when she'd explained why she had followed her father's orders to break off their relationship. It had been the self-loathing when she had described herself as prone to running away. He remembered how many times she'd mentioned feeling weak and submissive during their summer together. Those first two months he'd witnessed it plenty of times himself. David Waldsworth had considered employees beneath him, mere insects compared to his greatness, so he hadn't bothered to hide his treatment of his daughter. What had it mattered if the hired help witnessed the cruel things he said? How many times had he wanted to come to Alexandra's defense as her father had lambasted her by the pool for not being friendly enough to a business associate or chastising her for not achieving a spot on the Dean's List for her spring semester?

Except as he remembered those moments, unfortunately now with stunning clarity, he was also confronted with an even harder question: Why had he dismissed all of that when Alexandra had broken things off with him? He had known how cruel David could be, seen it time and time again. He'd also seen how frantic and upset Alexandra had been the night before. Why had he let her go?

His arms tightened around the woman sleeping peacefully in his arms. He'd blamed Alexandra all these years. But what if, in the end, the person most at fault was him?

CHAPTER FOURTEEN

ALEXANDRA ADJUSTED A stalk of snapdragon before standing back to survey her work. A glass vase full of spring blooms adorned each picnic table, and the mix of lavender freesia, pale pink roses, magenta pieris and orange carnations added vivid color to the backyard, a pleasing contrast against the lush green lawn and the white beach house in the background.

Her eyes drifted up to the balcony before she yanked her gaze away and turned to face the water. Waves rolled in, crashing and tumbling onto the sand toward the grass, then smoothing out and slowly receding into the ocean.

She'd woken up in the circle of Grant's arms, snuggled deep into the warmth of his chest. They'd walked back to the mansion after the second time they'd made love. He'd carried her up the stairs, stripped her once more of her dress and tumbled her back onto his bed, where he'd worshipped her body again before they'd collapsed in each other's arms.

The perfect place to wake up and watch through the blinds as the darkness of morning gave way to the soft pastels of dawn. As she'd started to wiggle away, Grant's hold on her had tightened and he'd pulled her

back against him, murmuring something in his sleep
before placing a kiss to her forehead that had made her
melt back into the bed.

As she'd given in to temptation and surrendered to
his embrace, her head resting on his chest as the familiar, comforting rhythm of his heartbeat thudded gently
against her cheek, she'd revisited her revelation from
the night before.

She was in love with Grant. She might have convinced herself those first few days that she had stopped
loving him, but she'd been lying to herself.

The problem now, she realized as a salty breeze
came in off the water, was what happened next. She
saw more and more of the old Grant: the carefree smiles,
the thoughtful touches, the more relaxed approach to
life. Mixed with the qualities of the new Grant, like
confidence and determination. He'd become a truly incredible man.

A man on the verge of achieving something amazing with his career while she tried to save her tiny little
floral shop. A barely there florist with a felon for a father living in a studio apartment she could only afford
because of her stepbrother.

She'd grown so much in the past nine years. But was
she good enough for the man Grant had become? Did
they have a chance at starting over? She'd told him everything, bared her heart and all of her failures. She'd
taken away his chance to choose all those years ago
and he hadn't snapped at her or gotten angry, as he'd
had every right to do.

She hadn't trusted him. She hadn't been strong
enough for either of them.

But all he'd done, again, was love her. Held her

through the tears, reassured her, kissed her until she hadn't been able to stand not feeling him against her, inside her, the insatiable need to touch him overriding all of her questions and doubts.

Goose bumps pebbled on her skin as she crossed her arms against the sudden chill. It wasn't just her own insecurities holding her back from confessing how she felt. No, it was the worry that her father's past would hurt Grant's future.

Could she risk telling Grant how she felt? Risk him returning her love again only to have everything crumble once someone made the connection that she was Alexandra Waldsworth, daughter of one of the greediest and cruelest investment managers in New York?

"Miss Moss!"

Alexandra whipped around, brushing her hair out of her face as she smiled at the young woman walking down the stairs. She scrambled for a moment to come up with a name.

"Good morning, Miss Friedman."

Ellen Friedman returned the smile with a sunny one of her own. She couldn't have been more than twenty-one, a tall young woman with ebony hair that seemed to defy the sea breeze and fall in a smooth curtain down to her waist.

"These flowers are stunning," she gushed as she bounced over to one of the picnic tables and leaned over to smell a carnation. "I'm used to seeing bouquets of daisies and roses, but the arrangements you come up with are so beautiful."

"Thank you, Miss Friedman."

"Call me Ellen." Her hand drifted up and she tucked

a strand of hair behind her ear. "I actually had a question for you. I'm getting married this fall."

"Congratulations," Alexandra replied with genuine happiness. She'd only encountered the graduate student a couple times over the past few days, but each time the young woman had been friendly and sweet.

Ellen's smile grew.

"Thanks. We're getting married at the Rainbow Room."

Alexandra's eyebrows climbed. The skyscraper that anchored the infamous Rockefeller Plaza in Midtown offered up its sixty-fifth floor to brides with stunning views of New York City, including floor-to-ceiling windows that overlooked the Empire State Building.

"That's incredible."

"I can hardly believe it." Ellen's sculpted eyebrows drew together as she frowned. "But I just found out my florist is expecting a baby a week before, and her assistant isn't comfortable taking over." She gestured to the flowers. "I've loved everything I've seen you do this past week. I know it's a longshot, you probably book years in advance, but is there any chance you'd be free to do my wedding?"

Alexandra barely contained the cautious thrill coursing through her veins as she pulled her phone out of her pocket. Another client and another wedding. At this rate she'd be able to break her lease and find a new storefront by the winter holidays.

"When is the wedding?"

"The first weekend in October."

"I'm actually free, so I'd—"

Ellen squealed and launched herself at Alexandra, wrapping her in an enthusiastic hug.

"Oh, thank you! I actually like your flowers much better. My mother picked the first florist, and she was nice but so traditional and just not Gary and me at all. I know you're swamped with helping Mr. Santos this week, but as soon as you're free, I'd love to set up an appointment with you."

Alexandra couldn't help but laugh. Was it too much to hope for, that she'd finally paid her dues and was emerging from the shadows of the past into an incredibly happy-looking future?

Ellen chattered on about her vision for her wedding as they walked back to the house and into the kitchen. Two of Pamela's chefs hurried about, cooking pancakes and filling pitchers of orange juice. Judging by the rumbling of conversation from the dining room down the hall, many of the other guests had come down for breakfast.

"I love this house," Ellen said as she snagged a glass of juice off a passing tray. "Mr. Santos is so fortunate he got it. Dad said it was quite the bidding war."

"It is stunning."

Amazing, though, Alexandra thought as her gaze drifted down the hall toward the dining room, searching for a familiar tall, dark-haired figure, that details like the vaulted ceilings and transom windows overlooking the hedged lawn and sunken tennis court no longer mattered. None of it would matter if Grant wasn't here to transform it from an incredible mansion to a home.

Her lips curved up as confidence surged through her. No matter what, she would tell him today how she felt. It was time for her to prove to herself, and him, that she was strong enough to believe in them.

She turned back to see Ellen watching her with a glow in her brown eyes.

"So how long have you known Mr. Santos?"

Her confidence ebbed as warning slid down the back of her neck. How was she supposed to answer? She didn't want to lie, but she didn't want to risk any of Grant's past with her father coming to light.

"Not long. We met once, years ago, but we only just became reacquainted last week when he moved back to New York."

The brief sense of relief that she had successfully navigated her first test disappeared as Ellen edged closer and lowered her voice to a conspirator's whisper.

"Really? Because I could have sworn there was something between the two of you." She fanned herself. "The way he looked at you last night, it was like something out of a romance book. Gary's extremely sweet, but I thought Mr. Santos was going to burst into flames."

The warning erupted into a full-blown alarm that sounded off in her head. She and Grant had so much to discuss, from whether there was an *us* to what he wanted to share with people.

"No," she said firmly with a smile to take the sting out of the word. "Mr. Santos and I met one summer when I was in college, but that was a long time ago. He's very attractive," she agreed with a wink, "but he's just my boss."

The dejected expression on Ellen's face would have made her laugh if she hadn't felt like a cornered animal.

"Oh." Her eyes brightened. "Maybe he has a secret crush on you!"

Alexandra forced a chuckle. "I doubt it. He's not my

type, and vice versa. Can you imagine Mr. Santos and me together? I don't think so."

Before Ellen could continue her relentless questioning, a silver-haired man dressed in a white shirt and matching shorts appeared at the end of the hall.

"There you are, Ellen."

"Oh, hey, Dad. I'll see you later at the picnic," she said to Alexandra. "Thank you again!"

Then she was gone, leaving Alexandra in the darkened hall. She released a sigh of relief. Hopefully, Ellen wouldn't say anything to anyone else about her romantic suspicions. She would need to talk with Grant as soon as possible and tell him what had happened.

A door creaked behind her. She jumped and whirled around.

"Grant!" Her hand flew to her chest as she smiled. "Sorry, I didn't even see the door there."

In the dim light it was hard to see his expression. But she could feel the anger rolling off him in thick, palpable waves. She reached out, then stopped herself, her hand falling back to her side. It wouldn't do to be seen touching the man she'd just sworn she had no personal interest in.

"Is everything okay?"

"Come into my office."

She quelled the sudden spurt of panic in her belly and stepped inside. Grant shut the door behind her, keeping several feet between them as he moved to a window overlooking the side yard. Silence reigned between them. The distant clink of glasses and murmur of guest voices seemed magnified tenfold.

Then, finally, "You and Ellen became acquainted fast."

"She's nice." She frowned. "Are you upset because I agreed to do her wedding?"

The look he shot over his shoulder could have frozen Hell.

"Why would I be upset?"

"I don't know. It's the only thing I can think of since I haven't seen you since…" Her words trailed off as her face heated.

"Since we had sex?"

Panic morphed into a hard ball of nauseated forbidding that lodged in her chest. The coldness in his tone, the borderline loathing as he threw out the word *sex;* all of it set off alarm bells that something was terribly, dreadfully wrong.

"Grant, what is going on?"

He whirled around so quickly she stepped back.

"What's going on is that after the last few days, I thought things had changed between us."

Confusion swamped her.

"I… I thought so, too."

"Then why did I overhear you denying our past to Ellen? Don't lie to me." His voice was barely above a whisper, but the last four words whipped out with such ferocity she felt their sting from her head to her toes. "I heard every word. That we met once long ago? That I'm not your type?"

Her lips parted. "Grant, it's not what you think. I was worried—"

"I'm sure you were worried. Worried to be associated with the Brazilian immigrant? Worried that people like Ellen Friedman might not want to work with someone who carries on a romance with the man who used to mow her father's lawn and plant his roses?"

Her eyes burned as she reached out to him. "Grant, that's not at all how I feel about you. I told you why I said those things back then. But it wasn't how I felt."

His laugh was twisted, cruel and ugly. It shifted him from the man she loved into the icy billionaire she'd encountered in New York. Someone who was just like all the men she'd met who had made her appreciate Grant all the more that summer.

"Of course it's not. Nothing is ever how it seems with you, is it?"

"If you truly think this little of me, why did you hire me in the first place?"

He leaned down, the harsh gleam in his eye making her stomach drop.

"I hired you to show you that you were wrong. That I achieved success, worth, wealth, everything you said I wouldn't." His eyes narrowed. "And yet I failed, didn't I? Since even the lowly florist barely scraping by still sees me as less than her equal, still not someone worth the dirt on the bottom of her shoe."

The pain in her chest as her heart broke anew was almost unbearable. This wasn't her Grant, cynical and untrusting. Yet, she shared some of the blame for this transformation. If she had been stronger all those years ago, they wouldn't be standing here now, with the past coming back to rip them apart.

"Grant, this is just a misunderstanding."

Another sardonic laugh escaped his lips. "How can I believe you?"

He couldn't, she realized as she barely kept her tears in check. There was only one way for this to go.

Her fingernails bit into her palms as she curled her hands into fists, steeling herself for what needed to be done. Her heart cried out, begged her to find another way, to not let the past win.

But there was no other option. And she was tired. She was so very, very tired from running from the past.

"You can't."

The only indication of his surprise was a blink.

"Then I was right."

She shook her head at his monotone.

"No. No, you weren't right." She looked over his shoulder at the lush green grass of the lawn. "I fell in love with you nine years ago and I never stopped. But my inability to stand up to my father kept us apart then, and unfortunately, it seems like it was a mistake that has doomed us permanently."

The weight of his stare pressed on her, making it difficult to breathe. She wanted to throw herself in his arms, to beg for one more chance at a happily-ever-after. But she could never ask that of him. If she truly loved him, she needed to let him go.

"I told Ellen that we didn't have a history because I wasn't sure what you were comfortable with me telling people. I also wasn't sure if her father would continue to do business if there was any hint of you being connected to a Waldsworth."

"That was nine years ago, Alexandra."

It was her turn to laugh, all the years of pain and heartbreak twisting the sound into something wretched and bleak.

"Yes. Nine years that you've held on to your anger with me and turned into a hard man who will never trust my word again. Rightfully so," she added, holding up a hand as he opened his mouth to say something, most likely a list of reasons as to why he deserved to be furious with her. "Nine years that a woman held on to a grudge against my father and denied me a lease for a store. Nine years that I've been in love with you. Nine years is nothing when pain is involved. My father hurt a lot of people, and I will always pay the price for looking the other way."

Grant took a step toward her.

"His actions are not your fault," he growled. "I've told you that repeatedly."

"You have. But my own actions—not standing up for you and for us when I had the chance—that was all me, Grant." She sucked in a deep breath and then walked to him. His body went rigid as she reached up and laid a hand on his cheek. The heat of his skin seared her palm, made her ache to feel his embrace one last time. She would have stayed in bed just a few minutes longer this morning if she would have known it would be the last time she'd lie next to him.

"What just happened now, your real reason for hiring me…" She swallowed past the ache building in her chest, spreading throughout her body. She hadn't thought it possible to hurt any more. But knowing he hadn't hired her because she'd impressed him with her hard work, her skill, was just another stab to her shattered heart. "You'll never be able to fully trust me. I see that now. Or to believe that I love you, that I won't turn around and run away when things get tough. We've both changed. You're a chief executive officer and all the other titles you wanted so much." The smile she gave him was full of grief for what might have been. "I'm just a florist. We don't belong together. Not anymore."

He caught her wrist in an iron grasp.

"That is not—"

A knock at the door cut him off.

"What?" Grant barked.

"There's a Mr. Simon on the phone for you from the Met." Jessica's voice didn't waver. "I wouldn't interrupt, sir, if it was anyone else."

Grant looked down at Alexandra.

"Don't leave. We have a lot more to discuss."

The command saddened her even as it rankled. Exhaustion dragged her body down into a high-backed chair as Grant released her and left the office, closing the door behind him. She was so very tired. Tired of the past always catching up; tired of people telling her what to do; tired of not standing up for herself and doing the right thing.

You can do the right thing now.

She mentally ran through her list. Today's picnic was the final event before the Hamptons guests returned to the city. The flowers were set out. If Pamela would take care of packing up the flowers and delivering them to the local hospital for patients' rooms once the event was concluded, then Alexandra could leave. Pamela would want answers later, but she would do it.

Because whatever Grant had to say to her wouldn't matter. Whether he agreed that their little fling was over or, in her wildest dreams, convinced her to stay, the result was still the same. He'd never be able to truly forgive her, never be able to stop wondering if she truly loved him. They would be caught in an endless loop of incredible, passionate highs and horrifying, heartbreaking lows.

He deserved better. She did, too, despite all her faults and mistakes. Being stuck in a relationship where the past would always be lurking in the background wouldn't be full of love and joy. It would be hell.

She grabbed a notepad off his desk and jotted a quick note. As she slipped out of the office and walked up the back stairs to her room, she texted Pamela to make arrangements for the flowers. Focusing on her to-do list helped keep her mind off the fact that her patched-up heart was once more breaking into tiny pieces, pieces she would never be able to put back together again.

As she neared the top of the stairs, her focus still on her phone, she missed the last step and tripped. She stumbled forward and caught herself on the wall. She looked down and almost gave in to the sudden, hysterical urge to laugh as she looked at her bare foot and then back at the shoe lying on the floor.

Had she imagined herself as Cinderella just days ago, a princess in a fairy tale where true love conquered all? She kicked the other heel off, snatched them both off the floor and hurried down the hall to her room. She placed the shoes in the closet and peeled off the dress, reaching for her jeans and T-shirt.

Fairy tales weren't real. True love certainly had no place in her life. If she wanted to move forward, she would have to close the door on her foolish dreams for a happily ever after once and for all. Which, she acknowledged as she stuffed her items into her suitcase, meant saying goodbye to Grant Santos forever.

CHAPTER FIFTEEN

GRANT GLANCED DOWN at his phone for what had to be the dozenth time in the past hour. The screen remained dark. He squelched the urge to tap out a text. It had been three days since he'd returned to an empty office and a brief note from Alexandra.

A very brief, professional note. He'd pulled it out and read it over and over again until the paper had turned soft with crinkles running through the loopy cursive.

Mr. Santos,
    Staff with La Meilleure will take care of flowers from the picnic. I will collaborate with Laura and Jessica on arrangements for the Met gala.
    Moving forward, a strictly professional relationship would be in both of our interests and the interests of our respective companies.
    Thank you for the opportunities you've provided me.
    Sincerely,
    Miss Moss

Anger had curled through his veins, hot and furious. Miss Moss? She dared to sign "Miss Moss" when just hours before she'd dashed off that note she'd been moaning his name and raking her nails down his back as she'd arched her hips against his thrusts.

He yanked open his desk drawer, threw his phone in and slammed it shut. He'd realized almost as soon as he'd revealed his reason for hiring her that the most logical explanation was the one Alexandra had just given; that the whole situation was a misunderstanding, a misguided attempt to protect him. As he'd left to take the phone call, he'd even started to formulate an apology for jumping to the worst possible conclusion.

Except she'd left. Fled rather than stay and talk to him. Again.

He scrubbed a hand over his face as he leaned back in his chair. How could he blame her for leaving? He hadn't given her a chance to explain. He'd jumped down her throat and said horrible things. Just as she had nine years ago, except she had been trying to protect him and his mother. His words had been born out of nothing more than pride and a feeble attempt to protect his heart.

To add salt to a very deep wound, he'd walked up to her room twenty minutes later to find her gone and every piece of clothing and jewelry he'd purchased left behind.

Including the sage green gown.

Desgraçado, he cursed himself.

Why had he ignored everything screaming at him that she truly was the same kind, thoughtful woman he'd fallen for?

No, he amended. The woman Alexandra had become was even more intoxicating than the Alexandra he had fallen in love with all those years ago. Young Alexandra had been sweet, loving and passionate. The grown-up

Alexandra still had those qualities, but she was more confident, self-assured. More herself.

He'd made a catastrophic error employing Alexandra for the sake of retribution. He should have turned her away when she'd arrived at the Pearson Group with that ridiculous arrangement, never let her set foot in his office. But his own fatal fixation on revenge had backfired in spectacular fashion. Alexandra hadn't just risen to the challenge, but she'd seduced him once more with her tenacity, her thoughtfulness and, in light of her confession yesterday, her bravery and selflessness. She'd turned the tables on him and proved herself without even trying.

He stood, restless energy sending him on the prowl around his office. Once it had been a symbol of his wealth, of everything he'd accomplished. Now it felt like a cage of his own making. He'd accrued millions, and for what? For his mother to live in a small home she treasured more than any beach house or faraway villa he could buy. For people in New York he barely knew to curry his favor.

The one thing he'd accomplished, taking down the cartel, had been a victory. But it hadn't brought him the peace he sought.

The only time he'd felt truly happy during his time in the United States had been with her. And he'd ruined it.

Movement flickered on one of the security cameras. Finn walked off the elevator and crossed to Jessica's desk, a flower arrangement in his hands. Grant's eyes snapped to the elevator just as the doors swished shut on the empty car.

He watched as his event manager, Laura, came out of her office and examined the arrangement, before she gave Finn an approving nod. He flashed a friendly smile before walking back toward the elevator.

Grant was on his feet and moving to his door before he could stop himself. He walked into the lobby just as the elevator doors were opening. He followed Finn into the car, ignoring the younger man's stare as he pushed the button for the tenth floor where one of the building's numerous coffee shops resided.

He didn't want coffee. He didn't need any more frantic energy zipping through his veins. What he should do was get off the elevator, even if he looked crazy for hopping on then off.

But he couldn't. Finn was a connection to Alexandra. And right now he needed a connection to her, craved it more than anything.

The doors closed. Lilting music filtered out of the speakers, a pleasant contrast to the tense silence that thickened the air. Now that he was here, he didn't know what to say. Should he ask after Alexandra? Keep his questions strictly business and see if Finn volunteered any information? He'd gone to bat against *Fortune 500* executives, warred with international moguls... And now he couldn't even string a sentence together.

The elevator hit the fortieth floor before Finn finally broke the silence.

"I was with her when she lost the baby."

Emotion punched him hard in the gut. The only outward sign that he'd heard Finn was his sudden intake of breath. But inside he ached: for the baby he'd never known, for the pain Alexandra had faced, both physically and emotionally. The heartbreak in her voice, the anguish in her eyes when she'd told him, had stirred up the sharp feelings of regret that had always lurked in the back of his mind. Feelings he had ignored to his own, and now her, detriment.

He closed his eyes as the elevator continued its descent. He'd accused Alexandra of repeating her past behavior. But wasn't he doing the same? Letting her go when he knew, deep in his soul, that there was more to the story?

"Thank you."

He opened his eyes to see Finn staring at him with a mixture of pity and irritation, a combination that stoked his banked anger. His first inclination was to snap at Finn. He didn't need pity from a man who had once sneered and laughed at him, who had fallen from spoiled rich playboy to lowly teacher.

He tempered it, swallowed his pride and forced himself to remain calm. The Finn he'd known nine years ago had changed drastically. While he might have fallen in the social ranks, so what? It had been hardworking teachers who had taught Grant English when he and his mother had arrived in the States; a high school math teacher who had found the scholarship that changed the course of his life. He had given in to his own obsession for prestige and money, come close to the same snobbery he'd despised in people like David Waldsworth, while letting some of the best parts of himself go.

And he genuinely liked the little bit of the new Finn he'd glimpsed that night in the bookshop. He certainly liked the man who had helped Alexandra in her darkest hour and kept her secret all these years.

"She told me that night that it was like losing you all over again." A fierce glower passed over Finn's face. "Said maybe it's what she deserved."

"What?" Grant snapped. "Deserved for what?"

"For not being strong enough to stand up to David. For hurting you."

"She was trying to protect my mother and me."

As he said the words out loud, something shifted in his chest; an acceptance of what had happened. Alexandra had been all of nineteen. Yes, things might have been different if she had come to him. But David Waldsworth had still wielded significant power back then. What if he had followed through on his threat and sent Grant and his mother back to Brazil? Perhaps his successes over the past nine years wouldn't have happened without Alexandra's sacrifice.

Regret burned in his chest. He'd wasted so much time on his foolish pride. But, he resolved, no more. He loved Alexandra, loved her more than he ever thought possible. They'd lost nine years. After his knee-jerk reaction to her conversation with Ellen, his unwillingness to consider that once more Alexandra had been trying to protect him, she might not want anything to do with him.

But this time he wasn't letting her go without a fight.

Grant let out a long, slow breath.

"How is she?"

"Miserable. Almost as bad as she was the last time. I think the only thing keeping her from wallowing away in her apartment is putting together the last of the pieces for your gala."

He ached to hold her in his arms, to soothe away the stress and tell her how sorry he was.

"I love her."

"And she loves you," Finn responded without hesitation. "So what are you going to do about it?"

The elevator dinged. The doors swished open.

A smile spread across Grant's face, his first real smile in days.

"I need your help."

CHAPTER SIXTEEN

ALEXANDRA STARED DOWN at the invitation on her desk. The embossed lettering glittered up at her, a sparkling reminder of the world she was no longer a part of.

Her fingers traced the S in "Santos." It wasn't the money or name brands or fancy cars she missed. No, it was the man she had fallen in love with not once but twice.

She swallowed past the tightness in her throat. How many people went an entire lifetime without experiencing the kind of love she had? How many would give anything to feel, just for a moment, the way Grant had made her feel? And here she was, on the verge of finally finding some stability with her dream career, moping and wishing for something else.

Was she still the same selfish, spoiled girl she'd been all those years ago? The one who had been too afraid to give up what she'd known for the unknown?

Her phone dinged. She picked it up, her heart plummeting as she read the text from her stepbrother.

Hey, sis. We had an offer to see a wedding venue tonight. Any chance one of your new employees could help with the delivery? I'm sorry, I'll make it up to you!

Seriously? She hadn't told Finn what had transpired between her and Grant in the Hamptons, but when she'd asked for him and Amanda to take care of setting up the flowers at the Met, he'd looked at her like he'd understood.

She sucked in a deep breath, then another, slowly calming her racing heart. Whether she liked it or not, she hadn't told Finn. He wasn't the one to blame.

She was. She'd been so hurt that Grant had jumped to the worst possible conclusion after eavesdropping on her conversation with Ellen. But then hadn't she proven him right? Instead of staying and fighting, instead of giving him a chance to share his viewpoint, she'd run.

Her eyes drifted back down to the invitation. No longer an innocuous piece of card stock, it taunted her, challenged her to prove to herself that she had truly changed. She wasn't under her father's thumb anymore. Nine years ago, even though fear had certainly played a part in her decision to give in to David's demands, she had genuinely believed herself powerless to stop him from sending Grant and his mother back to Brazil.

She had no such excuse now. Now she was allowing fear to rule her decision making.

The silver cursive flashed in the sunlight streaming in through the front window of her shop. The shop that would only be her home for another week before she moved into a new space just a few storefronts down from The Story Keeper. Harry Hill and his wife, Lucy, had visited her store and, after Lucy had tactfully inquired whether Alexandra was happy with her location, had offered her a lease on the spot for one of their numerous properties.

The brief rekindling of her romance with Grant may

have gone down in flaming glory. But at least the rest of her life finally seemed to be sliding into place. A life she had worked hard for, risked so much for.

Wasn't Grant worth one more risk?

Determination strengthened her spirit. She would conduct herself as a professional and deliver the flowers, set them up, make sure that Grant's final event went off without a hitch. And, before she left tonight, she would tell him she loved him. If his fury in the Hamptons was any indicator, he wouldn't reciprocate with loving words of his own.

But she owed them both the truth. Owed him the knowledge that he was worth more to her than her fear.

She picked up her phone before she lost her nerve and texted back.

Not a problem. I'll take care of it.

Little bubbles popped up, disappeared and then another text appeared.

Great. Tonight's your night, sis.

She bit back the urge to laugh. Yeah, tonight would be a night to remember. If things went the way they had in the Hamptons, orders would be rolling in to The Flower Bell faster than she would be able to keep up. Toss in a new location in Greenwich Village and she would be set.

It would be the thing that kept her going after she offered up her bruised and battered heart for a third and, hopefully, final rendering.

She texted back with a smiley face that mocked the ache growing inside her chest.

Yeah, maybe you're right.

Alexandra wiped her palms on her pants as she glanced nervously around the grand hall in the museum. The gala wasn't supposed to start for another hour. The setting sun's rays lit up the hall and highlighted the reds, pinks, corals and ivories of the arrangements she'd created for tonight's event. The bright colors gave a nod to the spring season, while the timeless elegance of roses and peonies reinforced the Pearson Group's image: innovative and fearless, but also trustworthy and classy. Once the lights were dimmed and the silver votives lit, the flowers would pop against the backdrop of black tablecloths.

Her gaze darted around the hall, her heart thundering in her chest. She'd expected Grant to be there, overseeing every last detail. But she'd only seen Pamela's catering staff and Jessica, who marched around in her impossible stilettos wielding a tablet like a shield and her pen like a sword.

A sigh escaped. It was better this way. Dumping something as large as an apology entwined with a confession of love right before one of the biggest events of Grant's career was poor timing at best, and selfish at worst. Perhaps she could follow up with him next week, bring him a congratulations bouquet and tell him in the privacy of his office.

Or you could be a big girl and tell him you'd just like to talk to him instead of finding an excuse.

She brushed away the pesky internal voice and started to walk away.

"Miss Moss!"

Jessica's voice cracked across the hall with the power of a lightning bolt. Alexandra turned slowly, half expecting Jessica to smack her on the back of the hand with the tablet. Truly, the woman had missed her calling as a drill sergeant.

"Yes?"

Jessica surveyed the tables with a critical eye. Had she thought Grant was the one she needed to impress? He might make the occasional recommendation, but it was the people like Jessica, the people who ran so much of what happened behind the scenes, that could make or break a business like hers.

Jessica's head snapped back around and she stared at Alexandra for a moment. And then she did the last thing Alexandra expected.

She smiled. A true smile that softened the harsher lines of her face and transformed her statuesque beauty into jaw-dropping gorgeousness.

"This looks wonderful, Miss Moss."

"Th-thank you."

"I was skeptical when you first came to the Carlson. But you've taken these events from cold, sterile presentations to warm, inviting events. Exactly the kind of atmosphere Mr. Santos, Ms. Jones and the other executives wanted to create for his clients." She glanced down at her watch. "Ms. Jones is taking care of a small emergency with the entertainment hired for the evening, but I sent her pictures of the arrangements. She's very pleased and would like to visit with you at a later date about upcoming events for the Pearson Group."

Alexandra returned her smile even as her heart jumped at the thought of continuing to work for Grant's company. She could do it, she told herself firmly, even if it hurt like hell.

"That means a great deal coming from you, Jessica. I know your standards, and Ms. Jones's, are exceptional. Meeting them makes me feel very proud of The Flower Bell."

Jessica arched a brow. "Which is great. But you should feel proud of yourself, too."

Warmth flooded Alexandra's chest. She'd often disassociated from The Flower Bell, referring to it instead of herself, afraid of developing the kind of ego that had led her father down his dark path. But, she acknowledged as she shook Jessica's hand, she'd poured a lot into her career. She'd worked hard, and her hard work was finally paying off.

"Thank you."

One perfectly sculpted eyebrow arched. "You've been good for him, too."

Alexandra outwardly froze, her effort to keep her face neutral at odds with her heartbeat accelerating into a gallop. "What?"

"He's more relaxed. Approachable. The Pearson Group is my third startup. He's very intelligent, as you know. But I worried that his focus on achieving his version of success would deter clients. I like the Mr. Santos I've seen the past couple weeks." Jessica grimaced. "Minus the sullen, grouchy fool he's been this past week."

A reluctant smile tugged at Alexandra's lips despite the ache building into her chest. She missed him. She missed his sharp wit and intelligence, his dry humor and encouragement. He was the only person who had never discouraged her, who had always told her she could do whatever she set her mind to.

"I messed up, Jessica."

The admission slipped out before she could stop it. But it was time; time to stop hiding behind who she used to be, behind her fears and self-loathing.

"It takes two, Alexandra." Jessica surprised her again by laying a comforting hand on her shoulder. "I wouldn't write off the past just yet."

With those enigmatic words hanging in the air, Jessica turned and marched off, the clicking of her heels echoing off the soaring ceilings.

Before Alexandra could begin to dissect what Jessica's cryptic message meant, her phone dinged. She pulled it out and frowned at the unfamiliar number.

Double-check the flower arrangements in the rooftop garden.

Perhaps Jessica had given her number to one of the museum staff? Or maybe Laura Jones had shared it with a member of her team. With a resigned sigh, Alexandra headed to the elevators. She wanted nothing more than to go home, sink into her old-fashioned claw-foot tub and relax in a warm bubble bath as she talked herself through how she would contact Grant and what she would say.

But she'd already netted several new contracts, including two weddings in addition to Ellen's, a New Year's Eve party and an anniversary celebration, which would keep The Flower Bell running long into the next year. Her initial goal of boosting the shop's profile had worked. Time to follow through, even if she felt like a tornado whirled inside her chest.

The elevator swooshed up, the doors opening to the Cantor Rooftop Garden Bar. Long white tables had been set up with matching chairs decorated with delicate strands of ivy. Café lights had been strung above the tables, creating an intimate glow against the backdrop of the greenery of Central Park and the New York City skyline standing proudly against the slowly pinkening sky as the sun began its descent toward the horizon.

Pride chased away some of the chaos reeling through her body. Small glass bowls full of roses offset by tiny clusters of white blooms softened the atmosphere of the cocktail tables. They also made sure the bouquets on the dinner tables, clusters of snapdragons, freesia, scented geraniums and other blooms with Brazil's national flower, the yellow ipê flower, at the heart of the arrangement took center stage.

When the sun set, the votive candles were lit and the lights of New York sparkled in the background, it would be perfect. She'd arranged to have the photographer, who would be floating around the event, take photos she could share on social media and her website later.

A quick walk-around revealed nothing wrong with the flowers. They stood tall and proud, leaves lush, petals unfurled into full bloom.

Probably just an overeager assistant, Alexandra thought as she walked back toward the elevator.

She pushed the button. Nothing happened. With a dejected sigh, she pushed it again. Still nothing. She walked over to the door that led to the stairs. The door stayed firmly shut.

Great. She was stuck on the roof of the Met Museum

in jeans and a T-shirt with less than an hour before the
event of the spring kicked off with some of the wealthiest prospective clients coming up in their finest couture
to party the night away.

All under the discerning eye of the man she loved
and whose heart she had broken not once, but twice.

Her heartbeat kicked into overdrive as she turned
and looked around for an escape. Perhaps there was a
fire ladder or some other way down.

Awareness whispered across her senses and sank
into her skin. She inhaled and his subtle, sensual amber
scent surrounded her.

"You locked the doors."

"I did."

His deep voice rolled through her body and filled her
veins with its seductive warmth. It took every ounce of
willpower not to whip around and throw herself into
his arms, bury her face against his neck.

"You don't need to sound so smug."

She kept her eyes on the luxurious towers that comprised Billionaires' Row at the southern end of Central
Park. The blue glass panels of one of the skyscrapers
glittered under the golden glow of the setting sun, lights
winking on in the various windows as people continued on with their lives, oblivious to the drama playing
out just a couple miles away. If she kept her attention
focused on anything but the man behind her, maybe
she would make it through this encounter without em-
barrassing herself.

"I'm anything but smug right now."

The thin thread of vulnerability in his voice, almost, but not quite masked by his gruff tone, cut her to
her core and ripped her from the present into the past.

Back to a library filled with expensive books that had hardly been touched aside from a daily dusting by the housekeeping staff, a diamond chandelier turned up to a blinding brightness and her father sitting in his favorite straight-backed leather chair, his hands resting on the armrests as if he was seated on a throne.

Details she had fixated on to avoid the crushing pain flickering in the eyes of her lover. Pain replaced by cold, hard contempt when she'd stood her ground and echoed what her father had told her to say.

I don't love you. I never did. You were just a fling.

The words still tasted bitter on her tongue. Uncertainty crawled beneath her skin, settling in the pit of her stomach like a coiled snake about to strike. She'd caused him so much pain over the years. Was telling him now how she felt the right thing to do? Or was she setting him up for more heartbreak?

"You ran away."

His statement held no acrimony or accusation. More an observation, a probe.

She sucked in a deep breath. She owed him so much, including the truth.

"I did run away." She swallowed hard. "I'm sorry. I…" Another deep breath, and then she summoned every ounce of strength she had as she turned to face him.

God, I miss him.

The sight of him hit her like a freight train. He looked so unbearably handsome dressed in a burgundy dress shirt, sleeves rolled up to his elbows, displaying his tanned forearms. Arms that had cradled her so tenderly, had made her feel simultaneously strong and cherished.

His black tuxedo pants were fitted to his muscular legs, stylish yet sexy.

And his face… Her fingers ached to trail over the strong line of his jaw, the sharply cut cheekbones, the broad swath of his forehead and into his thick black hair, smoothing the lines that had formed at the corners of his eyes as she told him that no matter what happened between them, he had done it. He had achieved everything he'd told her he would and more. She ached for the pain he'd suffered even as pride sang through her veins at all he had overcome.

How could he not see what an incredible man he'd been over the years, from novice gardener and aspiring entrepreneur to successful business professional? Would he ever see himself the way she saw him? Or would he always see himself as he had that horrific night in the library: a failure, a reject?

She steeled herself against her body's reaction to his presence. He'd brought up the topic of their relationship. She might as well say what she'd decided to say. Let the cards fall and, when he rejected her as she'd rejected him, she could go home and comfort herself with a hot bath and a very large glass of wine.

"I have some things I need to say."

CHAPTER SEVENTEEN

GRANT DEVOURED ALEXANDRA with his gaze, his eyes seeking out every detail he'd missed since he'd last seen her. The strands of dark mahogany hair falling from her ponytail and lying gently against her neck. The small upturn to her nose that added a hint of mischief to her beautiful face. And, most of all, the determined set of her lips, an outward sign of the strength she'd developed over the years. He'd loved her that summer, fallen so deeply in love he had never stopped loving her.

But the past couple of weeks, getting to know the woman Alexandra had become, had made him fall in love with her all over again. It wasn't just her courage but her compassion, her grace, her ability to find light in darkness. That she'd remade herself without any help from her father's legacy made him love and respect her all the more.

"I have some things I need to say."

Cold fear wrapped around his heart and squeezed. She'd said similar words nine years ago. Had he imagined what was developing between them? Or had he ruined it by jumping to conclusions and lashing out from pain and shame?

"As do I. Ladies first."

She bit down on her lower lip. The sight heated his blood as he remembered her lips closing around him, driving him to within an inch of losing control. His hands curled into fists. It was the only way he stopped himself from reaching out and pulling her against him.

"I apologized recently for being a coward all those years ago. And then I turned around and behaved cowardly again."

Her voice caught. His heart tore.

"No, Alexandra, it wasn't—"

"Don't make excuses for me." She turned away and walked to the wall of the garden, crossing her arms against a light breeze, her back ramrod straight. "When you thought I had rejected you again, I was so hurt. Even a little angry."

I know.

"But how could you not think that of me?" He could feel the doubts overtake her, saw it in the droop of her head, hear it as her voice dropped to a self-deprecating whisper. It cut through him like a knife. "After I let my father ruin what we had…after I didn't stand up for us…"

He closed the distance between them in seconds. His hands wrapped around her waist, spinning her around to face him. Her lips parted in surprise just before he cupped her face in one hand and kissed her.

He poured everything into his kiss: his love, his regret, his passion, his hope. For a moment she didn't respond and his grip on her tightened. If she turned him away, if it was too late, at least he would have this one last moment.

And then she came alive beneath his touch, her mouth opening to his caress, her arms wrapping around his neck as she pressed her body against his and moaned his name.

He wanted nothing more than to keep kissing her, to imprint his touch on her and claim her as his once and for all.

Soon.

He pulled back and rested his forehead on hers, gratified that her breath was just as harsh and fractured as his.

"Alexandra, you were nineteen. You were nineteen and innocent and under the thumb of an abusive, manipulative man." His hands slid around to her back and he pressed her close, wishing he could absorb all the pain David Waldsworth had caused her over the years. "I knew something was wrong that day. I knew you better than anyone else, and I walked away." His voice roughened as he tilted her chin up so she could look him square in the eye. "*I* walked away. I left you. Because I was hurt and embarrassed and let my damn pride keep me from seeing what was really going on. I left you, and carrying our child…" He paused, swallowed hard. "I left you both to that monster. And now, when I had a second chance at a future with you, I nearly let that same pride chase you away again."

Her hands flew up and clasped his face, tears sparkling in her eyes.

"Don't you dare take responsibility for this. I made mistakes, too."

He threw back his head and laughed.

"Are we going to stand here and argue about who is more at fault, or are you going to let me tell you that I love you?"

Her eyes widened as a cautious hope brightened their hazel depths.

"You…you love me?"

"I never stopped. Is it too much to hope that you—?"

She jumped and wrapped her legs around his waist, burying her face against his neck as she began to cry.

"Alexandra…"

"They're happy tears!" She leaned back and gave him a smile so radiant it rivaled the lights of New York City. "I love you, Grant. I love you, and I came here tonight to tell you. I know I'm stronger and more capable, but if I couldn't take the risk of telling you how I felt, then none of what I've done the last nine years matters—"

"It matters," Grant interrupted hotly. "Alexandra, the woman you've become, all the things you've accomplished—"

"Hey, the same applies to you!" she interrupted, her brow furrowing. "How dare you question what you've built? You've done everything you ever set out to achieve. The Pearson Group is going to be a monumental success and one of the most trusted financial firms in the city."

"But also one that puts people first." He kissed the tip of her nose. "Because of you. I had become so fixated on numbers, on milestones, that I nearly became what I hated. I wanted the title of billionaire so badly while you were barely scraping by and still making donations to the victims' fund."

Alexandra ducked her head, a becoming blush stealing over her cheeks.

"How did you know?"

"Your stepbrother told me."

She frowned. "Finn? When did you talk to…?" Her

voice trailed off and she muttered something under her breath. "That little toad! He was in on this whole thing, wasn't he?"

"Not the spoiled brat I used to think him. He was very amenable when I asked how best to get you here." He pressed his forehead against hers. "It's also when he told me all the incredible things you've done over the years."

Twin spots of red bloomed in her cheeks.

"Donating was the right thing to do."

"And I love that about you." He pressed another kiss to her forehead. "It's why I made a donation to the fund and brought the total compensation up to one hundred percent yesterday."

Alexandra's mouth dropped open. "But that…that was several hundred million! What about your billion-dollar goal?"

"I'll reach it someday. This was more important than some arbitrary benchmark." His fingers slid into her hair, gently combing through the silky strands. "You make me want to be the man you fell in love with that summer, Alexandra. To be worthy of your love."

Fear flickered across her face as she unwrapped her legs and slid down his body. He sucked in a breath, willing himself to stay focused on their conversation.

"I don't feel worthy. I feel…scared."

"Scared?"

"Scared I'm going to let you down again. Or myself. Or both."

He kept one hand in her hair, the other resting gently yet possessively on the back of her neck.

"Do you love me, Alexandra?"

"With all my heart."

"And I love you. One of the mistakes I made that summer was putting you up on a pedestal, one so high you would have fallen off at some point. That was my fault, not yours," he said as she started to interrupt him. "Yes, you made mistakes, but I did, too. Yet, here we are, both willing to forgive, both still in love and, I hope, still wanting to move forward. Together."

Her lips slowly stretched into a smile.

"Together sounds very nice."

"Good." He released her and stepped back, then dropped to one knee. Her gasp filled him with pleasure as he reached into his back pocket and pulled out a small navy box. He flipped the lid to reveal a green tourmaline ring, diamonds winking up at them from silver roses carved into the band.

"Alexandra Moss, would you do me the honor of becoming my wife?"

She hesitated. "Grant, I want… Lucy Hill was so kind to me when she found out who I was. But what if there are others who aren't so forgiving? I don't want to hurt you."

"Then they're not worth a place in my life. Not if they can't see you for who you are." His voice softened. "Alexandra, you are one of the strongest people I know, if not the strongest. Don't let fear stop you now. We can do this. Together."

The last vestiges of worry eased from her body. Tears fell once more, but the smile that accompanied them made his heart nearly burst from his chest.

"Yes, Grant. I would be honored to be your—"

He surged to his feet and cut her off with a kiss that nearly burned the clothes from their bodies. His hands drifted down, cupped her rear and pressed her flush against his growing hardness.

"Grant… I want…your guests…"

"Damn." He glanced back at the closed door and then down at his watch. "Unfortunately, we don't have time to celebrate properly before they arrive. But I expect you to come home with me afterward so I can show you just how happy your answer has made me."

With a sly quirk of one eyebrow, her hand slid between their bodies and settled on his hard length, the material of his pants the only barrier between his body and her sultry caress.

"I noticed."

"Devil woman," he whispered with a playful nip at her lips. "Since we can't leave now, you might as well open your gift."

"You're more than enough," she replied with an answering kiss.

Reluctantly, he released her and moved over to the door to the staircase, unlocking and opening it to reveal a white box tied with a red bow sitting on the top step. He set it on one of the tables.

"Open it."

Alexandra gave him a shy smile that made him resolve to buy her a gift at least once a week, just so he could see the look of excitement on her face. It could be a seashell or a flower or a book. Knowing her, just the fact that he had thought of her would be enough.

But this, he knew as he watched her lift the lid with anticipation and brush aside the tissue paper, this was something even more special.

Alexandra's mouth dropped open as she pulled the sage green gown from the box.

"Grant…it's…"

"Yours."

Her gaze flew up to his, tears making her eyes glisten. "You bought everything for me, didn't you? The dresses, the jewelry?"

"Yes." One hand came up, his fingers tracing the curve of her face. "You deserve so much, Alexandra."

She held the gown up against her body, her fingers drifting over the smooth crepe fabric in wonder.

"Jessica included something in the bottom."

"Jessica was in on this, too?" Alexandra chuckled. "I never…" Her voice trailed off as she pulled out a pair of transparent heels studded with tiny flickering diamonds. "I can't believe she remembered. I didn't even think she was really listening."

"She was. She told me she knew you would put the money you were earning back into your business instead of spending it on yourself. It was one of the many things she listed as a reason for why I needed to do whatever it took to get you back when I told her what I had planned for tonight."

He moved to her, savoring the heat that kindled in her eyes as she looked up at him.

"I would be honored if you would wear the dress, the shoes and the ring," he added as he pulled the ring from the box still clutched in his hand and slid it onto her finger, "when I announce our engagement tonight."

She started to laugh.

"Is this real? Or am I dreaming I'm in a fairy tale and I'm going to wake up?"

He pulled her close and lowered his head.

"As real as it gets. And not a day goes by that I won't remind you how lucky I am to have you in my life."

With that promise lingering in the spring air, he closed his lips over hers and claimed his runaway Cinderella with a kiss that let her know he would never let her go again.

EPILOGUE

Three years later

GRANT RAISED HIS head off the beach towel, a smile crossing his face as the soft babbles of his daughter reached his ears. Carla splashed happily in the shallow waters of the Atlantic as gentle waves lapped against the Brazilian beach. Alexandra sat next to her, scooping wet puddles of sand onto Carla's chubby thighs with one hand and adjusting their daughter's sun hat with the other.

The past three years had whipped by so quickly, sometimes Grant could hardly believe they'd happened. Their engagement had generated a surprising amount of positive press, and Jessica's quiet leaks to the media that Alexandra had been living off her own financial means and donating to the fund that had reimbursed her father's victims, along with Grant's own donation, had smoothed the majority of ruffled feathers. The few who hadn't been able to look past who Alexandra's father was had faded into the background. Grant had kept his promise; he had no interest in doing business with anyone who treated Alexandra like a second-class citizen because of the unfortunate stroke of fate that had seen her born to a man like David Waldsworth. Their intimate October wedding had been followed by the Christmas news that he was going to be a father. Seven months later Carla had entered the world with a healthy wail and beautiful green-gold eyes just like her mother.

He hadn't thought it possible to be any happier than he already was. But life with his wife and daughter had brought him more joy than he had ever experienced.

The Pearson Group had launched the night Alexandra had said yes to his proposal and quickly taken New York City by storm. Less than a year after its launch, Grant's personal net worth had soared past one billion dollars.

And he couldn't care less, he thought as he watched Alexandra pull Carla into her lap and press a salty kiss to her cheek. Alexandra had reminded him of who he used to be and what really mattered. Yes, the Pearson Group was important, but funneling money into causes they cared about, from establishing a fund for up-and-coming entrepreneurs in New York City to sending money to communities in Brazil, had become his focus. One that Alexandra, when she wasn't designing the latest wedding bouquets and centerpieces for the Big Apple's elite, helped him with.

That and making several trips throughout the year back to Brazil. Coming home, seeing his family for the first time in two decades, watching his mother blossom as she'd walked up and down the streets of her former home, had been a balm to his soul. The pain of losing his father would never fully heal. But with Alexandra by his side and the heat of a Brazilian sun warming his skin, life was better than he had ever thought possible.

Alexandra looked up, her eyes darkening as she caught Grant's gaze and gave him a saucy wink.

Thank God they had visited Brazil in the off season, when the beaches were all but empty. Otherwise, his body's uncontrolled reaction to the flirtatious smile lurking on her lips would be on display for the world to see.

"What time does your mother arrive?" Alexandra asked as she picked Carla up and bounced her on her hip.

Grant's eyes traveled over her trim frame encased in a ruby-red one-piece, her tan legs glowing under the morning sun. Legs that had been wrapped around his waist last night as he'd thrust into her, her body draped over the edge of the pool, head back as she'd tried, and failed, to keep her cries from escaping past her lips. A problem he'd been happy to solve as he'd kissed her and swallowed her moans of pleasure as he'd followed her over the top and into explosive bliss.

"Five o'clock. And Finn and Amanda and their brood arrive tomorrow. Between our little goblin and Finn's twins, my mother will be in baby heaven," Grant said with a smile as he sat up and held out his arms. His smile grew as Alexandra passed him twenty-eight pounds of wet, sandy toddler. Carla jabbered at him and wrapped her hands around one of his fingers.

"Maybe Carla would like to spend some time with her *Avó* Jordana tonight and we could go out for dinner."

He arched a suggestive eyebrow at her. "Is that code for something?"

Alexandra playfully swatted at his thigh as she sat down on a towel next to him. "No. I was just thinking we should take advantage while we can. It'll be a lot harder to go out when there are two kids."

"I can…"

His voice trailed off as her words sank in. His head whipped around, his chest expanding as he took in her radiant smile.

"You're…" His eyes drifted down to her stomach, then back to her face. "Really?"

"Probably close to seven weeks."

He reached over, snaked an arm around her waist, pulled her across the sand onto his towel and kissed her long and hard.

"I kiss Daddy!"

Grant pulled back just as Carla threw her arms around his neck and planted a sandy kiss on his cheek. Grant threw back his head and laughed as Alexandra snuggled into his side.

"I was wrong," he said as he kissed first the top of his daughter's head and then his wife's.

"Oh?"

"I think we're living in a fairy tale."

* * * * *

#4081 REUNITED BY THE GREEK'S BABY
by Annie West

When Theo was wrongfully imprisoned, ending his affair with Isla was vital for her safety. Proven innocent at last, he discovers she's pregnant! Nothing will stop Theo from claiming his child. But he must convince Isla that he wants her, too!

#4082 THE SECRET SHE MUST TELL THE SPANIARD
The Long-Lost Cortéz Brothers
by Clare Connelly

Alicia's ex, Graciano, makes a winning bid at a charity auction to whisk her away to his private island. She must gather the courage to admit the truth: after she was forced to abandon Graciano...she had his daughter!

#4083 THE BOSS'S STOLEN BRIDE
by Natalie Anderson

Darcie must marry to take custody of her orphaned goddaughter, but arriving at the registry office, she finds herself without her convenient groom. Until her boss, Elias, offers a solution: he'll wed his irreplaceable assistant—immediately!

#4084 WED FOR THEIR ROYAL HEIR
Three Ruthless Kings
by Jackie Ashenden

Facing the woman he shared one reckless night with, Galen experiences the same lightning bolt of desire. Then shame at discovering the terrible mistake that tore Solace from their son. There's only one acceptable option: claiming Solace at the royal altar!

HPCNMRA0123

#4085 A CONVENIENT RING TO CLAIM HER
Four Weddings and a Baby
by Dani Collins

Life has taught orphan Quinn to trust only herself. So while her secret fling with billionaire Micah was her first taste of passion, it wasn't supposed to last forever. Dare she agree to Micah's surprising new proposition?

#4086 THE HOUSEKEEPER'S INVITATION TO ITALY
by Cathy Williams

Housekeeper Sophie is honor bound to reveal to Alessio the shocking secrets that her boss, his father, has hidden from him. Still, Sophie didn't expect Alessio to make her the solution to his family's problems...by inviting her to Lake Garda as his pretend girlfriend!

#4087 THE PRINCE'S FORBIDDEN CINDERELLA
The Secret Twin Sisters
by Kim Lawrence

Widower Prince Marco is surprised to be brought to task by his daughter's new nanny, fiery Kate! And when their forbidden connection turns to intoxicating passion, Marco finds himself dangerously close to giving in to what he's always promised to never feel...

#4088 THE NIGHTS SHE SPENT WITH THE CEO
Cape Town Tycoons
by Joss Wood

With two sisters to care for, chauffeur Lex can't risk her job. Ignoring her ridiculous attraction to CEO Cole is essential. Until a snowstorm cuts them off from reality. And makes Lex dream beyond a few forbidden nights...

YOU CAN FIND MORE INFORMATION ON UPCOMING HARLEQUIN TITLES, FREE EXCERPTS AND MORE AT HARLEQUIN.COM.

HPCNMRB0123

Get 4 FREE REWARDS!

We'll send you 2 FREE Books plus 2 FREE Mystery Gifts.

FREE Value Over **$20**

Both the **Harlequin® Desire** and **Harlequin Presents®** series feature compelling novels filled with passion, sensuality and intriguing scandals.

HARLEQUIN
PLUS

Try the best multimedia subscription service for romance readers like you!

Read, Watch and Play.

Experience the easiest way to get the romance content you crave.

Start your **FREE TRIAL** at
<u>www.harlequinplus.com/freetrial</u>.